ATILUS THE SLAVE

CW01636997

To Leslie Flood

Edward Thomson

Atilus the Slave

Futura Publications Limited

A Futura Book

First published in Great Britain in 1975
by Futura Publications Limited
Copyright © Edward Thomson and
Futura Publications Limited 1975

This book is sold subject to the condition that it shall not, by way of trade or otherwise, be lent, re-sold, hired out or otherwise circulated without the publisher's prior consent in any form of binding or cover other than that in which it is published and without a similar condition including this condition being imposed on the subsequent purchaser.

ISBN 0 8600 71944
Printed in Great Britain by
Hazell Watson & Viney Ltd
Aylesbury, Bucks

Futura Publications Limited
49 Poland Street
London W1A 2LG

CHAPTER 1

They came with a tread which shook the world, the legions, the auxiliaries, bringing the greed, the cunning, the guile of Rome. Britain had gold, silver, iron, lead and tin. It could provide slaves and skins, corn and cattle, land and taxes. A rich prize hanging temptingly at the edge of the Roman Empire. In the third year of his reign Claudius sent Aulus Plautis to take it.

I was present at the end.

The Romans had overrun the south, taking London, fresh troops arriving under the personal command of the Emperor himself to continue the push to Colchester. Twenty miles from London Caractacus had assembled his troops in the great stronghold on Brentwood Ridge. If it was taken nothing could stop the Roman advance and Britain would fall, but to me, a boy of ten, it seemed impossible that we could lose.

My mother held the same opinion.

'If we hold fast, Atilus, then the Romans will have to attack and, when they do, we'll cut them to shreds. Once that is done the chariots will take care of the rest.'

'And if they go around us?'

'We'll cut their lines of communication and attack them from the rear. The result will be the same. Romans!' she spat into the fire. 'May the gods rot them all!'

She was of the Iceni, a handsome woman who had retained her figure, possibly because I was her only child. She had married when young, after a romance with an itinerant trader from Gaul. He had ingratiated himself into our tribe, making friends with the Druids, proving his worth with the news he carried as part of his wares. He dealt in knives, beads, glassware, trinkets; items of luxury which eased life in the mud and wattle houses. A slight, solemn-looking man, he had taught me Latin and Greek and had insisted that I learned to read. Against the burly warriors he had seemed insignificant, but my mother must have seen something in him, and he was kind to us both in his fashion.

My father. I looked into the glow of the embers remembering how he'd fallen silent whenever Rome was mentioned. A man of peace, he'd taught me none of the martial arts, that had been left to the friends I had managed to make. There'd been play with wooden swords and knives waved with more enthusiasm than skill as we'd run shrieking over the meadows. But we had travelled a little, he and I. Not far and not fast, visiting nearby tribes and once going as far as Colchester itself.

That had been last year, just before he had vanished, my mother breaking the marriage bowl from which they had drunk salted wine. She had divorced him for no reason I clearly understood. Perhaps it had been because he had given her no other child, or she could have suspected him of being an agent of Rome, reporting our weaknesses and strengths. A Druid had spoken with her just before she'd broken the bowl and, since then, she had never mentioned his name.

Leaning forward she blew gently on the fire, the sudden glow painting her face with crimson, her hair with ruby shimmers. It was long, oiled, hanging loosely over her shoulders. Her dress was of coarse wool, belted at the waist, a long dagger of bronze with a leaf-shaped blade carried naked for all to see. Like the men she had painted her face with woad. Like the men she would fight.

'Atilus, you'd better get some sleep now.'

'I'm not tired.'

'Then just lie down and rest. Not here, go and find a place somewhere else.'

She blew again at the embers and I knew she wanted to be alone. Perhaps to fashion a spell against our enemies or to perform some other magical rite. The women of the Iceni knew things which no man was permitted to learn.

Rising I moved into the darkness, stepping carefully over sleeping figures. Other fires made dim points of light all around, men lying between them, fully dressed, broadswords and shields close to hand. In their compound the horses snorted, restless, soothed by their grooms. The chariots were ranked, ready to be harnessed, attendants waiting on the nobles to whom they belonged.

It was hard to rest. I was tired, overstrained from our journey and the night was full of odd noises. I heard a peculiar trumpeting and the dull beat of something which sounded like drums. There was a scurry as if birds winged through the night and, from the woods, came the hoot of an owl. Closer to hand men muttered in their sleep, twitching, one suddenly crying out.

'The fire! The fire!'

A dream, at such times all men had dreams, visions of what was to come. As the man settled, snoring, I wondered what message had been sent to him from the gods. What message would be sent to me.

If any came I remembered nothing of it. Barely had I closed my eyes and it was dawn. The day had broken full of mist which quickly cleared from the vicinity of the stronghold but which lay like a thick veil over the river and the enemy camp. All around was the stir and bustle of activity as men woke, stretched, gulped down a hasty meal prepared by the women.

My mother had mine ready, a mess of lumpy porridge lacking salt and tasting of smoke. As I cleared the bowl voices rose from the horse compound and a line of chariots moved towards the opened gates.

'Mother?'

'It's Caractacus,' she said, narrowing her eyes. 'He's leaving. Run after him and see what's happening.'

I passed through the gates, dodging a guard who tried to stop me, joining a group of warriors. Other chariots stood further down the line, those belonging to King Cattigern of the Trinovent. He and Caractacus seemed to be arguing. I had sharp ears, a few steps closer and I could hear what was being said.

'This is madness. Why have you deserted your position?'

'Are you accusing me of cowardice?'

Caractacus was coldly polite. 'Is there any other reason for you withdrawing your troops?'

'The gods are against us. Somehow we must have offended them. All night my commander has been coughing and, an hour before dawn, he spat blood.'

'Then make an offering.'

'I have, two horses, but the position is doomed. Surely you can see that? A man cannot fight against the gods. I have no choice but to withdraw.'

There was nothing Caractacus could do. He ruled by consent and not by force.

My mother cursed as she heard the news.

'We can't hold the stronghold without Cattigern. And if we run the Romans will overwhelm us. Caractacus will have to attack before more fools take fright at omens. May the gods be with us this day!' Reaching out she pulled me close to her, holding me tight. 'Atilus, my son, take care.'

'You too, mother.'

'Yes.' She recovered her composure; tears could only weaken a warrior and, though young, I was a man. 'Now listen to me. If the worst should happen make your way to Colchester. Wait in the sacred grove to the north. If I do not join you in three days go home and place yourself under the protection of my uncle. You understand?'

'Yes, mother.' I was anxious at the thought of being

parted. 'But you won't let anything happen to you, will you?'

'We are in the hands of the gods,' she said bleakly. 'Get to the horses now, they'll be needing your help with the chariots.'

The chariots which we hoped would smash the might of Rome.

They filed out with the nobles standing straight and proud, the reins wrapped around their waists, spears and lances ready to hand. Like an avalanche they thundered down the slope leading to the mist-shrouded Roman camp and, like an avalanche, they broke.

Horses went mad as they caught the unfamiliar stench of camels, rearing, screaming, tangling the reins and overturning the chariots. Others fell, caught by the trip-ropes stretched in the tall grass, team piling on team, necks and backs breaking, wood splintering, the air filled with shrieks, screams, the cries of injured and dying men and beasts.

Then came the devils, Nubians painted and ghastly as they rose from where they had been hidden, spears stabbing at the fallen, the warriors who had run after the chariots.

The guile and cunning of Rome struck superstitious terror into the hearts of our men, sending then running in panic, easy prey for the legionaries.

From the upper slope I watched as they advanced, spreading, killing, accoutrements flashing in the sun, shields blazing, swords glimmering, red cloaks aping the colour of the blood they spilled with such careless ease.

Men of the legions which ruled the world.

A warrior came running towards me, fell as a pilum thudded into his back, the shaft of the spear like a wand rising above his body. Another tried to make a stand, his broadsword a wheel of light. It's edge was useless against the hemispherical shield, his own no defence against the calculated thrust which sent steel into his belly. Doubled, vomiting blood, he fell.

As did others, the slopes covered with them, the very grass turning from green to red.

I ran.

The woods were thick and the undergrowth a good place in which to hide. I found a small hollow beneath a tree, one covered with bracken, and burrowed into it like the terrified animal I was. I felt sick and my stomach was knotted with fear, muscles jerking to every sound. The air was full of sound, yells, hoarsely shouted commands, the shrieking of the women as they ran, bare-footed, hair streaming, to stab and run to strike again.

The day grew older, the sound of battle fading as the legionaries pursued the broken forces as they ran towards Colchester. If my mother had remained alive that is where I would meet her, in the grove of sacred oaks to the north of the town. We would return home, there to live quietly, perhaps to fight another day. It was important that I didn't keep her waiting.

Leaving my hiding place I moved cautiously through the woods until they thinned to open country across which snaked the dirt path of the road. It was wide, rutted, littered with dead who lay like discarded rag dolls. The air held the taint of newly shed blood, a heavy, sickly-sweet odour which caused me to retch.

Straightening, wiping my mouth, I heard the voice.

'Hold there!' It was harsh, the snapped command in Latin. 'You, boy, stand where you are!'

There were three of them, coming at a fast trot from the woods I had just left. A party sent to take care of any stragglers they might find. For a moment I stared at them, my feet seeming to have sunk into the ground and then, with an effort, I turned and ran into the bushes at the side of the road.

'Butuus, after him!'

'A boy?'

'You know the orders. Get him!'

One of the three came running, the others following close behind. I could easily have lost them, armed and armoured as they were they had no chance of catching me in a race, but as I turned for a final look behind my foot caught against something soft and I went sprawling.

Rising I looked at my mother.

She was dead, raped, her legs straddled, blood between her thighs. Her face was turned, one cheek against the dirt, more dirt in her hair, her clenched hands. Her wrists were torn and dark with bruises. The dress had been ripped to expose her breasts and a patch of blood showed where a dagger had been thrust into her heart.

There had been no need to hurry. She would not be waiting at the sacred grove.

I had a dagger myself, a small thing of sharpened iron. I drew it, backed a little and, as the leading soldier came close, flung myself at him.

It was as if I'd attacked a stone wall. The knife was useless against his armour and he gave me no chance to reach his face. Contemptuously he knocked me down, kicked the blade from my hand, hauled me upright with a hand locked in my hair.

'Look what I've found,' he said as the others joined him. 'A regular savage. The swine tried to knife me.'

'Then cut his throat and let's get moving, Butuus,' said the eldest of the other two. 'We've no time to waste on vermin.'

'Kill,' I said in Latin. 'That's all you Romans think about. Pigs! Filth! Why don't you leave us alone?'

'Watch your mouth, boy!'

The blow almost knocked me unconscious and I would have fallen if it hadn't been for the hand locked in my hair.

Blood ran from my cut lip, falling to spatter on the ground to stain the edge of the torn dress.

Dully I said, 'Did you have to kill her?'

'The woman?' The eldest legionary glanced at where she lay. 'You know her?'

'My mother.'

'I see.' He sucked in his breath, frowning. 'Those bastards of the fourteenth,' he muttered. 'One standing on her wrists while the others took their pleasure. And the Emperor Claudius gave strict orders against it. That's why they had to kill her in order to shut her mouth.' His tone sharpened a little. 'What's your name, boy?'

I strained against the hand holding my hair.

'Let him go, Butuus, but stand close. Now, boy, what is your name?'

Wiping the blood from my mouth I said, 'Atilus Cindras.'

'That's a Roman name. Is your father a Roman? Look up when I speak to you. Is he?' I felt his hand under my chin, saw his face as he lifted mine. It was deeply creased, the nose large, the eyes brown, deep-set beneath the rim of his helmet. He smelt of sweat and garlic, leather and oil. 'Well, is he?'

'I don't know.'

'You don't know your own father?'

'He was a trader from Gaul. I haven't seen him for a year. I think he's dead.'

'You think?'

'I hope. If he was a Roman I'm ashamed to be his son. You Romans!' My voice began to break despite my resolve to hold it steady. 'My mother – you didn't have to do that to her. She . . .' I gulped, conscious of the stinging in my eyes. 'She . . .'

'Let it out, boy,' he said kindly. 'Don't try to hold it in. Cry if you want to, the gods know you've reason enough.'

I stiffened, biting my lip. A warrior of the Iceni did not cry.

'Well, lads?' He looked at the others. 'What do you think?'

'He tried to kill me,' rumbled Butuus.

'He'd just found his mother. Look at her. Can you blame him?'

'Well, no, but we didn't do it.'

'As the boy can testify if it comes to that.' The third man spoke for the first time. His voice was thin, cutting, his accent bad. His face was swarthy and scarred with pockmarks. 'It's the only real proof we have if someone finds the body and reports it. The Emperor's orders were plain and he's a man of his word. He'll execute anyone found guilty of breaking them. Also he's fond of making examples.'

'So?'

'The boy speaks Latin and good Latin at that. His father could be a Roman citizen, quite a few of them settled here. That's reason enough for taking him in.'

'He said—'

'I know what he said, Butuus, but we don't have to believe him. He's a witness and, anyway, he might fetch a decent price.'

'A boy?'

'One who speaks Latin.'

So it was decided as I stood looking at the dead body of my mother. Ants were running over her face and into her staring eyes. She had died defending Britain. Now I was a slave of Rome.

CHAPTER 2

The captives were herded into the stronghold, prisoners in the very place which, if held, would have given them safety. The women were separated from the men and squatted, keening, their hair over their faces, blood running from the flesh they had torn with their nails.

The men were crushed, broken, many wounded, convinced the gods had turned against them. Among them were a few boys, all older than myself, and one of them joined me where I sat as a soldier yelled something from beyond the stockade.

'What's he saying, Atilus?'

Cymbelle was of my own tribe, but we had never been friends. The son of a noble he'd had little time for the offspring of a trader, but now his father and uncle were dead, his elder brother somewhere on the road to Colchester. He might escape to freedom, but Cymbelle would not. Now he was eager for any familiar company.

'Atilus?'

'He's asking about feeding us,' I said. 'And he mentioned water.'

'They'll poison it.'

'No.'

'You can't be sure,' he insisted. 'It would be a quick way to get rid of us.'

He was ignorant for all his nobility, but I'd had the advantage of a father who knew how Rome operated.

'If they'd wanted to kill us they would have done it when we were taken,' I said patiently. 'We're war-captives now, slaves. As such we're worth money to Rome. They'll feed us and the water won't be poisoned.'

He scowled, barely convinced and more than a little afraid. He had been hurt, a minor wound on his left arm, and blood was oozing from the cut. I tore a strip from his tunic and bound it tight over the gaping flesh. He thanked me and continued to talk.

'I could have got away,' he muttered. 'When the chariot overturned I was lucky. The reins snapped and I was thrown clear. I should have stayed where I'd fallen and pretended to be dead. A chance would have offered itself – but there was not time to think.'

He touched his arm, wincing.

'Caractacus ran towards Colchester, I saw him go. Perhaps he'll make a stand somewhere down the road. We could even be rescued.'

He was dreaming, hoping when there was no hope, but he was a noble and I said nothing. My silence unnerved him and he left me to wander among the others. I was glad to be alone.

The afternoon ended and from all sides came cries from the wounded as they suffered from thirst. The women had stopped their keening and sat moaning instead, the sound eerie and frightening. Some of them committed suicide by swallowing their tongues. A few ripped open veins with their jagged nails. The rest sat and waited as did the men.

There was nothing else to do.

At dusk the Romans gave us water, taking a party of twenty men to haul it from the river, but they gave us nothing to eat until well past the following dawn. It was a mess of sour porridge and we ate it with our bare hands, using fingers to thrust it into our mouths. For a week nothing else was given us but water at dusk and porridge in the morning. The compound in which we were held stank of urine and excreta and several men died of their wounds.

I would have starved if it hadn't been for a guard.

Mucius was a grizzled veteran with scarred thighs and a

snaggle of broken and rotting teeth. His breath smelt and his eyes were yellowed, the lower lids inflamed, the lashes and corners speckled with dried pus. He was in charge of the party delivering the food and he had noted my smallness. Noted too that I stood little chance against the men whom hunger had made savage as they fought over the buckets.

'What's your name, boy?' He grunted as I told him. 'So you're the young devil who tried to knife Butuus. A pity you didn't make it, the swine still owes me five denarii from a dice game. Hungry?'

'Yes.'

'Like something nice to eat?' He chuckled at my expression. 'Don't look so scared. I'm no Greek after your rounded young bottom. Go outside and wait.' He added, casually. 'Try to run and you'll maybe get ten yards then you'll be spitted like a goose.'

He took me to where fires blazed under suspended pots and gave me bread, oil and a scrap of honeycomb. As I ate I looked around. The Roman camp had extended itself up the slope and legionaries seemed to be everywhere. Men were busy at work piling broken chariots and other damaged equipment into a great pile on a stretch of level ground.

'They'll be burned as an offering to the gods,' said Mucius. He had watched the movements of my eyes. 'Still hungry?'

He handed me another wedge of bread and I learned why he had been so generous.

'You move around in there,' his head jerked at the compound. 'You're young and they wouldn't notice if you edged close. You might be able to learn things. If you hear anyone planning anything let me know, eh?' He winked. 'It'll just be between the two of us.'

'You want me to be a spy?'

'I want to avoid trouble, boy. The best way to stop it is before it starts. I'll put you on the food detail, that way they won't suspect anything and you'll get a chance to eat before those wolves snatch it all. If they ask why you were ordered outside tell them that you were questioned about your mother. Three of the fourteenth have been arrested for rape – they die tomorrow.'

That night, when I dreamed of my mother she was smiling.

I didn't see the executions, but I heard the trumpets and though I doubt if the men had killed my mother it helped to think they had. At least, afterwards, I slept easier though the food may have had something to do with that. I made no attempt to act the spy and I don't think Mucius expected me to, it was probably an excuse to justify his generosity in case of need.

Ten days after our arrangement the prisoners were sorted. Tables had been set up outside the compound and small groups taken out at sword point to answer questions. Those who held a high position or who were the sons of chiefs or nobles were offered the chance to buy their freedom, but first they had to swear loyalty to Rome. Cymbelle was one of them. He didn't look towards me as he burned a pinch of incense at the altar and gave his oath.

The rest of us were to be shipped to Gaul.

Mucius was one of the guards conducting the party. He was a decanus in charge of ten men and was close to having served his thirty years. Because I was no real threat he allowed me to walk beside him, a thong around my neck attached to his wrist. If I made any attempt to escape a jerk would bring me down, choking.

The other captives were also held at the neck, each man attached to others by a yoke in groups of five, an arrangement which left them free to walk but made it impossible for them to make any attempt to gain their freedom.

At night we camped, the yokes held by ropes fastened to stakes hammered into the ground, and Mucius talked.

'This seems a fine country, Atilus. I've half a mind to settle here when I'm released. I could open a wine shop in London or Colchester and take things easy. A wife to take care of things, a slave, maybe to do all the hard work, what man could wish for more?'

He belched over his bowl of wine.

'Take Germany, now. That's where I did most of my service. Forests so dark you could walk in them for months and a barbarian behind every tree. We've settled the Rhine and things aren't too bad there now, but the winters are hard. I remember one time when I went to relieve a man on guard we found him frozen as stiff as a board. You couldn't stand still a minute if you didn't want to stick to the ground. I've seen men who had to cut boots from their feet before they could move. Do you get winters like that?'

'Not often,' I admitted. 'But it gets damp.'

'That's bad.' He helped himself to more wine from a skin he'd managed to sneak into the supplies. 'Damp can hurt the bones and make a man creak when he tries to stand. I'm too old for that. Just give me a little comfort and I'll be happy. Spain, now, the sun is hot there like it is in Capua. That's where I was born,' he explained. 'A decent city and a fine arena.' He fell silent, brooding, staring into his bowl. 'Damned woman,' he muttered. 'She was a real hell-cat.'

'Your wife?'

'My mother, step-mother that is. My father was a fool. He could have fixed himself up with a nice young slave girl, but he had to get ambitious. She had a little property of her own, a widow with a snot of a son, and he thought it would be smart to combine what they had and go into business. He had as much idea of trade as I have of flying and they skinned him. She never let him forget it, nagging all the time and making life hell. Finally he wound up taking care of the beasts at the arena. A nursemaid to a bunch of animals. I can smell them yet.' He stiffened. 'What's that?'

'A wolf.' I listened to the distant howling. 'It's calling for a mate.'

'Have you ever hunted them?' He answered his own question. 'No, of course you haven't, you're too young. We had some at the arena once. They broke out of their cage and attacked some bears then turned on the keepers. A couple had their throats torn out and another lost a hand. For a while it was as good as an actual event at the games, blood everywhere, then they called in the archers to take care of them. My father was blamed and had to pay for some of the damage. I thought my step-mother would go mad. That's when I left home and joined up.'

'Because she quarrelled?'

'Not exactly. I fetched her a crack with an empty amphora of wine and thought it best not to hang around.' Mucius threw the dregs of his wine into the fire. 'Well, I'd better go the rounds. You still hungry?'

'Yes.'

'Boys are always hungry.' He handed me a lump of cold porridge. 'Don't forget the water for the morning.'

I'd offered to bathe his eyes, he woke with them crusted and it was an effort to part the lids, but water warmed at the fire dissolved the dried pus and cleared the lashes. In a way it was serving Rome, but I liked the man and I needed the food he could give me. A weakness perhaps, but a small boy, alone, could not be blamed.

My mother did not blame me. That night she came even closer and I could hear her voice.

'Atilus, my son, live. Live to grow into a man. A boy can do little against Rome, but a man – live, my son. Live!'

A message sent with the aid of the gods who now watched over her. One I would do my best to obey.

We reached the coast where we were to take ship for Boulogne. Winter was coming and, with it, storms, yet the port was busy. More troops, officers coming to take over their command, couriers and with them a host of civilians and slaves; men to take care of accounts, others to win what they could from the new province.

Mucius reported to a tribune and was told to load us on a ship due to leave within the hour. It was a round-ship used to shift cargo, fitted with oars and a big, square sail. The oars were used when entering and leaving harbour, the sail when on the open sea. The master was annoyed at the extra cargo.

'The wind's wrong,' he complained. 'If it shifts we'll be in trouble. And I'm overloaded as it is.'

'If you want to complain don't do it to me.' Mucius was curt. He had expected to pass us over and return to his legion, now he had to take us on to Boulogne. 'I've got my orders.'

'Mine come from Neptune.'

'And mine from Aulus Plautis via his tribune. And he gets his from the Emperor. If you want to argue with him I don't. Now do we get moving or stand here all day?'

The voyage was a nightmare. Even though Mucius kept me with him I was sick most of the time and it must have been terrible for those locked in the hold. At Boulogne we were taken to an empty shed and given a meal of beans boiled with turnips and fragments of meat, some bread and a measure of vinegary wine. The man doling out the food hesitated when he saw me, but Mucius snapped, 'Give him the same as the rest.'

'A boy?'

'A war-captive of the Emperor and don't you forget it.' He had suffered during the voyage and his temper was short. 'Now get on with it and let's have less of your mouth!'

I didn't drink the wine but gave it instead to a man who had bruised his face when he had fallen in the hold. He took it without thanks and sat, brooding, for the rest of the night.

In the morning we were fed again, told to wash and then assembled for the inspection of the buyers. They thronged into the shed, some simply curious, others intent on purchase. Among them was a Greek with curled and scented hair, a burly man with scarred hands and a fussy little person with a cap which had flaps that could be lowered over the ears.

The Greek called out to him as he passed down the line.

'Don't take them all, Capaneus. Others have to make a living and we haven't all got the backing of the Statilius family.'

'I'll take what I need.'

'But why be so particular? Anything's good enough to provide a show.'

'That's why you're falling out of favour, Thalidies,' said the burly man with a laugh. 'More than one Master of the Games had told me that unless you provide better wares, they'll not waste their time dealing with you.'

'Perhaps.' The Greek shrugged. He had full lips and his fingers looked like worms. 'They'll change their minds when the crowd roars and contenders run short. Anyway, Brachus, a tip for your ear. I'm not going to Lyons this time. I'll leave the market open to you. Just remember the favour when I ask you to accommodate me some other time.'

'What favour?' Brachus scowled. 'The time you do anything to help me is the time I watch for a dagger in the back. Greeks, who can trust them? Hurry now, Capaneus.'

The agent made no comment. He stared at the man to whom I'd given the wine.

'What were you, chariot or sword?'

The man stared, not understanding the Latin. The agent frowned, suspecting insolence, lifting his hand to signal a guard who stood to one side. He held a whip with lumps of lead knotted into the thong.

I said, quickly, 'He doesn't understand you.'

He looked at me in surprise then said, 'But you do? Good. Ask him the question. What did he use in battle, chariot or sword.'

'Sword,' I said immediately.

'I asked him, not you.'

'The answer would be the same. He is not a noble and so would have owned no chariot.'

Thrusting himself forward the Greek touched me, his lips moist, his hands clammy.

'An unexpected pleasure,' he purred. 'A young boy who can talk a civilised language. I think I could use such a lad. Oiled, taught a few of the more tender arts, he could command a fair price in Antioch.'

'Greeks!' The burly man spat. 'You turn a man's stomach.'

'Careful, Brachus!'

'Why? I'm a Roman citizen and as good as any man who walks the earth. You want to bid for the boy? Then name your figure, but by all the gods you'll not get him cheap!'

His anger was real and I sensed a rivalry of long standing between the two men. Another of the buyers came forward, ran his hands over my shoulders, arms and body, stared into my eyes then shook his head.

'No. Taming him would take too long. You're a fool to consider him, Thalidies, he could do your client a serious injury.'

'Stick to the east if you want perverts,' advised another. 'That young barbarian can't be trusted. What do you know of him, decarus?'

'He knifed a legionary,' said Mucius stiffly. 'It took three to hold him.'

An exaggeration, but it worked. The Greek shrugged and turned away. Brachus remained, his eyes thoughtful. I saw him whisper to Mucius and coins changed hands.

Later, on the way to the auction block, Mucius trod

heavily on my foot. I was limping as I mounted the pedestal and a small, crippled boy was of little worth.

Brachus bought me cheap, but he didn't keep me for long. He sold me to a man who owned land and a villa in Narbonese Gaul.

CHAPTER 3

Publius Varus Severus was a tall, spare man in his middle forties. His shoulders were stooped, his lips thin and he walked with a slight limp; the relic of a wound he had received during military service. He was a widower with a son a year older than myself, his other, older son, having died three years earlier. It was for the sake of Macer rather than a need for slaves which made him interested in me.

His villa was at Vienne which lay to the south of Lyons where Brachus had disposed of the other slaves he had bought. We had travelled fast yet had been caught by the winter and I was cold and miserable as we were led into the house.

Severus prodded me as if I had been a horse.

'He's fit, Domini,' said Brachus. 'Strong bones and muscles and his teeth are sound. Open your mouth, boy.'

Severus nodded as he looked inside. He wore a heavy ring on his hand, the signet of a member of the equestrian order. A knight, he had great local influence and family connections in Rome.

'From Britain, you say?'

'Taken during the Emperor's campaign. He fought like a man and put up such a good show the legionaries spared him. As a soldier yourself, Domini, you can appreciate how they like a display of courage. He's a little wild, but can be tamed. And he speaks good Latin and knows Greek.'

'Greek?'

'Yes.' Brachus had been pleased at the discovery; it enhanced my value. 'And he's tough. He kept up all the time even though his feet were bleeding. You could use him in the fields, but he'd be of greater value in the house. It would be a pity to waste all that education.'

'Your name, boy?'

I told him and Brachus slapped my face.

'You address the Domini as "master",' he snapped. 'And your name is simply Atilus, a slave needs no more than one.'

The blow had been hard and I lowered my face to stare at the elaborate mosaics set into the floor of the atrium. It was a large chamber with glowing braziers set at intervals and a line of statues at the walls. The air was warm and scented with the tang of incense which had been burned before the household gods. There were couches and low tables set with vases of alabaster. The house itself was the largest I had ever entered and I wondered why, if the Romans had so much, they should be greedy for more.

Severus said, thoughtfully, 'He needs taming, you say?'

'Training, rather, Domini. The Britons are savages and unused to civilised customs, but he is young and will quickly learn. I thought of you as soon as I saw him.'

'The price?'

'Twenty gold pieces.'

'Ten. I could use the boy but the price of slaves has fallen and will drop even lower now that the Emperor has taken Britain. Take it or leave it, I am not inclined to haggle.'

Brachus took it and I entered the household.

I was house-trained, taught certain skills, even tutored after a fashion, but my main purpose was to fetch and carry and to attend Macer wherever he went.

As the years passed we grew close.

He was lonely, chafing at the restrictions of the farm, impatient to enter the life beyond. Though he was older than I was he had barely more growth, a lack he tried to make up with strenuous exercise. Together we chopped wood, swinging axes until our muscles ached, digging, running, leaping from tuft to tuft of the thick grass which grew in the western marshes.

I grew tall and strong. The food, though plain, was wholesome and the female slaves in the kitchens always had a little extra to spare. One of them, Celia, used to save scraps from the master's table, sharing them with me as we sat beneath the trees edging the slave quarters.

She was of Macer's age, a slim, dark-haired girl with a budding figure and was already conscious of her physical attractions. Some of the men had tried to get close to her and she told me about it as we chewed fragments of chicken and goose.

'Cilo tried to kiss me this morning,' she said casually. 'He said he loved me, but all he wants is to use my body. Do you, Atilus?'

'Love you?'

'Use my body, stupid. You know what women are for, don't you?' She bit into another scrap of meat. 'Is it true that before a fight all the British warriors lie with women? And if there aren't enough women to go around they share what is available?'

'No,' I said flatly. 'That isn't true.'

'How can you be sure? You were only a boy at the time. Anyway, you can't deny they fight naked and covered with paint.'

'That isn't true, either. Woad isn't paint.'

'It's close enough.' She shrugged and wiped her mouth on the back of her hand. 'Kiss me, Atilus.'

She was on me before I knew it, body pressing, lips rammed against my own. As a kiss it was clumsy, but I was young and couldn't help but respond. Laughing she pulled away.

'There, Atilus, you see? You're just like all the rest. Think of me the next time Macer takes you to the baths.'

The day was warm, but I felt a chill as I entered the

house. Celia had reminded me of things I had almost forgotten. The strongest grief can be eased by time and now the past seemed very remote. The life of the villa had enfolded me, kept me busy, softened me while it developed both body and mind. I was a slave and had accepted the life of a slave. Romans fed, housed and clothed me and, like a tamed beast, I no longer flinched at the touch of the hands which had made it captive.

For that Didius was partly to blame.

The tutor was an old man, a Greek, and he had been delighted to learn that I spoke his tongue, though badly. He had insisted that we speak it together when Macer was present and much to Severus's pleasure both he and I had gained proficiency in the language. He had given the old man a new woollen garment. I had received nothing, but I was only a barbarian while Didius was the product of a civilisation which had been old when Rome was young.

'The exercise of logic demands that we accept the inevitable, Atilus,' he told me when, one winter's day, we sat hunched before a brazier. Severus had taken Macer on a visit to the nearby town. 'You are a slave as I am and there has always been, and will always be, slaves. It is a fact of life like the sun rising in the east and setting in the west. Would you struggle against the wetness of the sea? Or the heat of summer, or the cold of winter? These things are and cannot be altered. To cavil against them is to set yourself against the gods.'

'Do you believe in the gods, Didius?'

'I would be a fool to say that I did not,' he said dryly. 'But there are degrees of belief as there are degrees of love. And what have you lost? In Britain you were a savage, here you share the comforts of civilisation. If you were freed tomorrow what would you live on? A wise man looks at the good things of life, he does not count his misfortunes.'

There had been more, skilful words to instil doubt in a

young mind, to errode previous convictions. Now I heard his voice raised as I entered the house. It grew louder as I passed into his chamber.

'Macer, attend! You will be considered an idiot in Rome unless you improve your rhetoric. Only a raw provincial would state his case in such an uncouth manner. If you ever become a senator you will be laughed from the Forum.'

Macer was stubborn, his cheeks flushed with anger.

'I don't want to become a senator. I'm going to join the army.'

'Even so—'

'You're a slave! I don't have to listen to you!' He turned towards me. 'Come on, Atilus, let's go and ride the horses.'

A slave also I had no choice but to obey. We rode for a while and then wrestled, stripped to the raw and throwing each other to the ground. I was the stronger and he exerted himself even more. By accident I struck his nose and he looked at the blood, his face ugly.

'You struck me! *You* struck me!'

'It was an accident.'

'Yes.' He stood, breathing deeply. 'Let's get back to the house.'

Severus was waiting; Didius had complained. The beating Macer received was only a token, the one given me was savage. My silence beneath the rod appealed to the knight's Stoic leanings.

'There is good in you, Atilus. A man should be able to bear pain without flinching. The discomfort of the body must not be allowed to disturb the calm tranquillity of the mind. You realise why you are being punished?'

'Master, I did no wrong.'

'That is true, but Macer must learn that his actions affect others. To insult his tutor was impolite, to defy my orders was unforgiveable. The next time he is tempted to disobey he will know that it is not he alone who will suffer.'

A form of logic with which I had no sympathy. Later, at the baths, when examining my weals, Macer laughed.

'At least, Atilus, you'll know what to expect if you join the army. Stripes are common.'

'I can't join the army. No slave can be a legionary.'

'Would you become one if you could?' Macer's eyes held a peculiar expression as if he held secret knowledge. 'Would you?'

'I might.'

'I want to know, Atilus.'

I couldn't understand his insistence, but it was easier to agree than to argue. 'Yes, but—'

'You can't be accepted until you are free,' he interrupted. 'I know that.'

He leaned back on the couch, sweating in the heat. With a strigil I scraped the dirt and oil from his pores, wiping the curved, bronze blade on a scrap of linen. An attendant slave scowled at me as he passed, taking me for a normal client robbing him of a tip.

'I'll have to do military service anyway if I hope to gain public office,' mused Macer. 'Father wants me to stand for election, but I think I'll stay with the army. When I'm the legate of a legion I'll show these armchair warriors just how to achieve victories. Earn a triumph too, maybe. Did you know that Aulus Plautius could claim a triumph if he wanted? He's killed more than five thousand of the British, that's more than the Emperor Claudius did and he was granted a triumph. You know, Atilus, the real power of Rome lies not in the Senate but with the legions. You'll see.'

I said nothing, finishing my scraping, then following him into the cold plunge where we sported for a while before he decided that he wanted his massage.

I used scented oils and my fingers dug deep.

'Careful, Atilus!'

'Sorry.'

After the massage we sat in the cooling room and listened to the gossip. Today it was of Messalina, the Emperor's wife. Claudius had finally discovered her flagrantly wanton behaviour and, after giving her a chance to commit suicide, had sent an officer to run her through with his sword.

The symbolism amused those present.

'I'll bet that's the first time she'd had something long and hard shoved into her and didn't like it,' said a fat, red-faced man.

Another laughed.

'Maybe she wouldn't have complained had he put it somewhere else.'

'Did you ever see her?' A lean man with a badly scarred leg hunched forward on his chair. 'She was a real beauty. I saw her once when I visited Rome, she was at the arena, you know, the one built by Titus Statilius.'

'The Taurus? Is that still standing?'

'Yes.'

'A good show?'

'Fair. I dropped in during the afternoon hoping to see some real action, but there was nothing special. They had a fairly good secutor and some of the bestiarii weren't too bad, but you can see as good at Lyons any day. That wasn't what I was going to tell you. Messalina was there with a few sychophants, among them a young lute player. Well, he was afraid of her, everyone could see that, and she kept threatening to throw him into the arena unless he did exactly what she wanted. I had a good seat and she didn't trouble to lower her voice so I could hear every word. The poor devil was sweating and he looked ready to throw a fit. She had a big gladiator with her and when she gave the signal he picked up the lute player by his feet and held him head downwards over the sand. He had long hair and it hung down like a woman's. A lion took a swipe at it and almost scalped him – he screamed as if he'd been gutted.'

'And?'

'He begged her to forgive him. When the gladiator set him down he dropped to his knees and kissed her feet. We could all tell what he had to do once they were alone.'

'I bet he regrets it now,' said the fat man. 'From what I hear heads are falling all over Rome. The woman must have operated like a brothel.'

Macer said, 'Why did she have to threaten anyone to make them go with her? If she was a beauty surely any man would have been willing.'

The lean man grunted. 'You're young, friend, but think about it. Would you commit adultery with the wife of the Emperor? A word and you'd find yourself tied in a sack with a boar. Or hanging on a cross. Or watching as they frizzled your genitals on a fire. No woman's worth it.'

'But how did she get away with it for so long?'

'The husband's the last to know,' said the fat man. 'Remember that when you're married.'

'But the Emperor! Surely someone would have told him?'

'Would you have done?' The lean man shook his head. 'It's taking a risk to tell any man his wife's acting the harlot, carry a tale like that to a man like Claudius and he'd accuse you of treason. He doted on her. You know what they say, no fool like an old fool, and he was old enough to be her father. He even gave orders to people that they should do exactly what she told them. Naturally he didn't know what her instructions would be – she certainly had him blinkered. Anyway, it's over now. Say, did you hear about that senator in Ravenna?'

The talk went on and it was late when we left the baths. Macer chose to take the long way back home and he headed to where the legion camp stood on a flat stretch of ground beneath a low hill. It was a training camp for new recruits and we could see a detachment returning from a route march. The setting sun threw gleaming reflections from their shields and armour and they made a fine sight as they passed. A tribune rode with them and he came trotting over to join us.

Tullius Voculus was just past twenty and already considered himself a veteran. He saluted Macer in the Roman manner.

'Come to look us over?'

'Just passing the time. Did you hear about Messalina?'

'Probably long before you did.' Voculus's gesture hinted that it was stale news and no longer of interest to an officer of the legion like himself. 'How is your father?'

'Well. We haven't seen you lately.'

'I've been too busy breaking in this batch.' The plume on the tribune's helmet nodded as he jerked his head towards the marching men. 'But I'll be around soon. I enjoy dining with your family and I've got some family news from Rome.'

Voculus was a distant relative of Severus and liked to keep in contact. In the army, influence could always help an ambitious man to rise, and the tribune was ambitious.

Looking at the marching column Macer said, 'How are they shaping?'

'Well enough, but they won't be true legionaries until they've faced the enemy. That'll weed out the failures and stiffen the rest. Come to think of it I've a punishment scheduled. I don't believe in keeping these things waiting; a quick show of discipline sets an example. It would do you good to watch. Teach you how men should be handled.'

Macer hesitated. 'It's late and I promised I would be home before dark.'

'You can't begin to learn too soon,' snapped Voculus. 'It's only a scourging and since when has a Roman objected to the sight of blood? Come on, now, you don't want to get a reputation for being weak.'

We rode into the camp and down the straight lanes between the tents and administration buildings. Any legionary could have found his way through any camp blindfolded, they were all built to exactly the same pattern. The man to be punished had been slow to obey an order, and when a centurion had beaten him with his vine staff, he had turned with an upraised hand. Had he struck the officer he would have been crucified, as it was the flesh would be torn from his back with lead-weighted thongs.

They did it with ceremony. The man was marched to the whipping post before the assembled men, his clothes ripped from his back as his hands were tied, a centurion calling out the reason for the punishment.

The horses shied at the first lash of the whip, with the scream they tore from the man's throat. I soothed them as I stood on the edge of the parade ground while the punishment continued. The first blows ripped the skin, those after gouged gobbets of flesh from the muscles below, blood running to puddle on the ground. The screaming died as the man slumped unconscious against the pole, but the scourging was continued until the white of bone showed in the crimson ruin of his back.

Macer joined me as bugles broke the assembly. He was white, his eyes strained.

'They've asked me to dine, Atilus,' he said. 'You'll have to wait outside with the horses as it will be dark by the time we're finished.'

He was swaying a little when he finally rejoined me and his breath reeked of wine. I helped him to mount and rode close beside him to catch him if he fell. Luckily the moon had risen early and gave a clear light so we made fairly good time.

Severus came from the house as we approached, warned by a slave. In the dancing light of torches his face was stern.

'Macer?'

'I'm sorry, father, but it couldn't be helped.' The ride had sobered him so that he did not stumble as he dismounted. Severus relaxed when he heard the explanation.

'And Tullius Voculus will come to dinner tomorrow? Good. It is time we heard the latest news of the legions. I shall order a sucking-pig to be prepared and open some of the best wine. But you should have sent Atilus to tell me what had happened.'

Dismissed I handed the horses over to the stable-slaves. It was late and I was hungry. The cook gave me a mess of cold vegetables and some bread which I dipped in oil. The slave quarters were dark; people who rose before dawn were ready for bed at dusk, besides which Severus was mean with oil for the lamps.

From the trees came a rustle and a low voice.

'Atilus?'

It was Celia. She came running forward, grabbed me by the hand and led me into the shadows.

'I was getting worried,' she said. 'I thought something might have happened to you. Are you hungry?'

'The cook gave me something.'

'And I can guess what. That fat old bitch treats the food as if she paid for it. Here, I saved you a piece of pie.'

It was good and I ate it sitting on the far side of the trees. The moon gave out a silver light and stars were bright in the sky.

'What happened, Atilus? Why were you so late?'

She sucked in her breath as I told her, making me repeat details, her lower lip full as I described the scourging.

'I've never seen a man flogged,' she said. 'And I've never seen a man bleed like that. What will happen to him? Will he die?'

'He might. It all depends on the way he heals.'

'But soldiers get wounded all the time and they don't

all die. Would you like to be a soldier, Atilus? You could kill men and take women and hold them and force their legs open and—'

'Stop it!'

'But wouldn't you like to take a woman and do that to her?' She pulled up the hem of her gown. 'Look at my legs, aren't they nice? Wouldn't you like to touch them? You can if you want.'

They were pale in the moonlight, tapering shafts joined with darkness, the skin soft and delicately downed.

'I've always liked you, Atilus,' she whispered. 'You're tall and fair and different to the others. Don't you like me? Wouldn't you like to kiss me?' Her lips came close. 'Wouldn't you, Atilus? Wouldn't you?'

This time it was different. Her lips were soft and warm, parting to emit her tongue, her arms lifting to close around my neck, holding me close so that I could feel the soft impact of her breasts.

And it didn't stop at a kiss.

She was afire and demanding fuel, kindling a similar flame in me, quenching it to fan it into greater life so that we rolled in a paroxysm of physical abandon until, finally, the flame was drowned.

Unsteadily I rose and, turning, looked into my past at a ghost.

She lay on her back, the gown pulled from her shoulders, her breasts exposed. Her legs were wide, joined with darkness which seemed to be blood. Her face was turned, shadowed as was her hair.

'Atilus?' She stirred. 'Come to me, Atilus.'

But I was running, crying, sick with shame.

CHAPTER 4

The following spring Celia had a child and claimed Cilo as the father. I saw it, a tiny thing, but its hair was black and the face looked nothing like my own. Serevus was no stranger to such events, unless all male slaves were gelded such things were bound to happen and the new life would grow into valuable property. He moved them to another estate and life went on as before.

Macer spent more and more time at the legion camp, going alone and sometimes spending several days at a stretch in the company of the officers. One day he summoned me and we went to a meadow in which stood a copse of trees. He carried thongs and told me what he intended to do.

'I've been watching the soldiers at their sword-drill, Atilus and it's obvious to me that a man has to be able to move fast in case of need. Voculus suggested a way to improve my speed. I want you to tie my hands behind me then lash at my face and body with a wand. To avoid the blows I'll have to dodge. We'll take turns.'

His blows hurt, mine were calculated to miss or barely touch. After an hour I was striped with weals, but the next day I was faster and after a few weeks I could duck, twist and turn like an eel.

Macer thought he was faster than he actually was and was more than pleased. Severus too, when he asked about our exercises, nodded his satisfaction.

'It is well that you are taking an interest in the military acts, Macer, but the camp would be a better place for that. I've agreed that you should stay there for a while to learn the duties of an officer. Voculus has asked that you be placed under him.'

'And Atilus?'

'Will stay here. It is time that he was taught how to keep the estate accounts.'

An excuse, no slave could be trained in martial arts, but Severus had been cunning. Macer left and I was placed under the supervision of Negrimus, an ageing man who snuffed and thrust his tongue between his lips as he frowned over the figures.

The following winter Didius fell sick. I visited him in his chamber, the brazier set at his feet doing little to dispel the chill. Wrapped in woollen garments he looked like one of the Egyptian mummys he had told me about. His eyes, deeply sunken, gave his wasted face the appearance of a begemmed skull. The hand he rested on mine was almost transparent.

'A man lives, Atilus, and he learns if he has any sense at all. Only a fool will ignore the advice he is offered and I do not take you to be a fool. Will you listen to me if I tell you something for your own good?'

'You shouldn't tire yourself. Leave it until you are well.'

'I shall never be well again and I know it.' His lips pursed in a thin smile. He spoke in Greek, mouthing the words as if relishing their taste and, for the first time, I wondered what he had been like when young. 'I am dying, Atilus, and so can afford to be brave. I have been watching you. You hate Rome.'

I said nothing.

'You hate being a slave despite all my lessons in logic,' he continued. 'But hate is a two-edged sword. Contain it and it will destroy you. Reveal it and you will betray yourself and the result will be the same. You are young and must learn.'

'Learn.' My voice was bitter. 'To take blows earned by another? To be meek when I would be proud. You can accept slavery, Didius, but for you it is different.'

'Because I am a Greek?' His head moved slowly from side to side. 'Do you think I love the barbarians of Rome? They came and they took as they always take. They made Greece a province of Rome as they have Britain, but we, at least, they respected for being what they hope to become. And did we really lose? Our culture still survives, the fruits of our civilization are living in Rome; one-time farmers who came to the Forum with mud on their boots and stinking of manure now wear silk and perfume. They watch the plays of Euripides and Sophocles. They discuss the philosophies of Plato and Socrates. In that manner Greece will survive. But you, Atilus, you must learn if you hope to stay alive. Metal, over-tempered, will snap when tested. You must be like the willow which bends to the wind. You must disguise what you feel.'

He was old and dying and deserved respect, yet I was young and with the blind convictions of my years.

'I do.'

'You did,' he corrected. 'Or perhaps, when little more than a child, you were stronger than you are now. You could even have accepted your fate. Then you changed. I would be interested to learn why.'

A woman lying in the moonlight, a ghost which had reminded me of what I had lost. But I could not tell him that and he didn't press the point.

'You are waiting,' he said, 'and you are becoming impatient. I can sense it if the others do not. Yet they are not blind and will recognize the danger. Do you want to die in the mines or at the oar of a galley? Heed my warning, Atilus, your life depends on it. Learn to act if nothing else.'

He died two days later and his passing left a gap. I had known him for almost half my life – I was not ashamed of my tears when they laid him to rest.

That summer Severus took Macer with him on a visit to Rome. He was eighteen now, and the old intimacy had gone, yet I had not wholly been forgotten. Before they left he came to me, smiling, a roll of parchment in his hand.

'Atilus, look at this! Father has given you to me. It's all signed and attested. Do you realize what it means?'

It meant I had changed hands like a horse or a sack of grain, but I smiled, remembering Didius's advice.

'It means that I'll be moving with you and, when you marry, take up a place in your household. At least I hope that's what it means.'

'More than that, Atilus.' His hand fell on my shoulder. 'I haven't forgotten the old days. Do you remember us talking once about the army? How I asked if you would join if you could?'

'No slave can join the legions, master.'

'But a freedman can. Don't you see, Atilus? I can make you free now any time I want.'

Free!

The thought made me dizzy so that I reached for a stool. To be able to go where I wanted, do what I wished, walk tall and proud as a man should. To return to Britain and rejoin my own people. I barely heard what Macer was saying.

'Thirty years of hard work, Atilus, but at the end you'll be a Roman citizen and be given a grant of land. We can join up together and I'll arrange for you to be with me. As a Tribune I'll be entitled to a man to look after my things. Imagine it, Atilus, we could even fight side by side, killing barbarians for the glory of Rome!'

Not free, then, but to change the status of a slave for that of a legionary, to continue to act as the servant for as long as Macer wished. I remembered the man I had seen scourged.

'Atilus?'

I smiled, overwhelmed at the offer, stooping to kiss his hands.

'Master, it's too much! I don't deserve such kindness.'

'Nonsense.' It pleased him to be gracious. 'Don't, Atilus.

There is no need for that. You have no need to lower your eyes.'

But it was safer for me to look at the floor, his sandals, the tiles on which he stood. Safer still to pretend ignorance about the procedure.

'But, master, how—'

'Simple,' he interrupted. 'First I'll go to the magistrates and free you. Then, when you have your certificate of manumission, we'll go to the camp and join up.'

This time I did not feign the smile. There would be a space of time in which I would be legally free and could do as I liked. The army would wait forever before I placed my neck in the yoke of the legion. I had accumulated a little money and would take passage to the coast down the river. Macer was being kind to me according to his way of thinking – I would be kinder to myself according to mine.

'When, master? When?'

'Not yet, Atilus. I'm going to stay with relatives for a while. Father thinks it important that I make myself known to the members of the senate and there are other obligations. You'll be staying here as you know.' Reaching up he dropped his hands on my shoulders. 'Be patient, Atilus, it won't be long.'

It might be months, perhaps years – with an effort I retained my smile.

'There's one other thing,' he added casually. 'Father is going to remarry. He'll be returning with his bride while I stay in Rome.'

Her name was Fulvia, a widow connected by her first marriage to the Claudian family, and I guessed the new union was a matter of politics. She was barely thirty and young enough to be Severus's daughter, a patrician and proud of her position and descent.

It was October when she arrived, the leaves were browning on the trees and a keen wind blew from the marshes. She stepped from her litter muffled in a heavy cloak and stood looking at the house and the house-slaves assembled to greet her.

Severus told her our names and duties as he led her past the line towards the door.

'Atilus? The keeper of the accounts?'

'Yes, my dear.'

She looked at me. 'Have them ready for me to examine in the morning.'

I bowed and she passed on. A small, rounded woman with a wealth of neatly curled hair, her features were clear-cut, the lips firm yet full, the chin rounded and dimpled with a cleft. Her eyes were blue beneath arched brows and her nose was thin, the nostrils slightly dilated, the bridge high.

Beside me Scipio drew in his breath.

'A looker,' he muttered. 'She'll keep the old man busy at night.'

'Us too,' commented the man on my other side. 'I know the type. We'll be dusting and polishing from dawn to dusk. Be clumsy at serving and she'll have the skin off your back. If you've been cheating on the accounts, Atilus, you'd better start praying to your gods. They may show you mercy, but she won't.'

Others had arrived with her; an older brother, Gratus Sabinus and a small girl, her only child. Lucillia was a pretty, pert little thing, spoiled and demanding. She was ten, the age I had been when I'd arrived at the house, but I had walked and she had been carried, I had been sold and she was a welcome member of the family.

Gratus Sabinus had a personal attendant, a scarred ex-gladiator whom he'd bought cheap from a lanista. Chilo had been lucky and knew it. He admitted as much to me when, later, we sat over wine in the kitchens.

'I was good for a few more bouts but my luck was running out. Meturus, that was my lanista, kept moving us around so

I hadn't the chance of building up a local following and these provincials don't appreciate the finer points of combat. In Rome, now, good sword-work is liked and a man has a chance if he puts up a decent show.' He emptied his bowl. 'Is there more wine?'

I gestured at the kitchen-slave and Chilo grunted as he poured from the pitcher.

'Gratus is a good man. Hard, but good. I'm useful to him and he knows it. It pays to have a trained man at your back when walking the streets at night. The lictors at Rome don't like us carrying weapons, but a man has the right to defend himself and a stave's as good as a sword if you know how to use it. In the provinces it's different.' He jerked his head towards the belt holding the gladius he'd carried on the journey. 'That's a good sword, well-tempered steel which holds an edge. You ever used one?'

'No.'

'Of course not, I was forgetting, you're a house-slave. What did you think of Flavia?'

'She looks a fine woman.'

'Don't be fooled by her looks.' Chilo burped over his wine, he was already a little drunk and in the mood to exchange confidences. 'She's part bitch and part wildcat and as selfish as they come. I like you, Atilus. You've got the body of a man even though that face of yours belongs on a Greek statue. Just watch yourself, understand?'

I poured him more wine, taking some myself but only pretending to drink. 'And the girl?'

'She'll grow up to be even worse. Always running around, spying, carrying tales. Watch what you say to her and guard your tongue when she could be listening. Now it's your turn. What are things like here? Any decent-looking women who might like to try a bout with an old gladiator?' His wink was suggestive.

I told him things he needed to know and finally put him to bed where he snored like a rooting sow.

As promised Flavia came the next morning to check my accounts. She wore an embroidered stola, her hair curled in ringlets which fell over her forehead, heavy with the scent of perfume. She was distant as she checked the figures, frowning at what she discovered. Severus was of the old school, the estate kept itself but made little profit.

I heard her talk to him about it afterwards.

'You have too many slaves, husband.' Her voice was clear but a little shrill. 'There isn't enough work to keep them all as busy as they should be. We could sell a third without loss to the estate. And you've got too many horses, the thing now is to go in for beans and wheat.'

'We get wheat from Egypt.'

'But never enough,' she snapped. 'You've let things slide and it isn't fair to Macer. Rome's expensive and he needs to entertain his friends. Gratus too, he should have a local appointment as duumvir. He's eligible and all he needs are the votes. You must think about these things, Severus.'

'I will, my dear.'

'When?'

'Later. In the spring.'

'That will be too late. The planting has to be planned and contracts found for the crops. If I don't mean anything to you then think of Lucillia. She's getting big and will need a dowry. I'm not having her marry some local farmer who can't trace his ancestry back more than a few generations. My family is descended from the Etruscans.'

'Lucillia's only ten, Flavia. Why talk of marriage so soon?'

'A mother has to plan ahead.'

'I will take care of her.'

'What as? A common knight? You should be a senator at least by now. If dear Clodius had lived . . .'

I heard Severus sigh and moved away as her voice, now strident, kept on.

It was but one of many quarrels which drove Severus from the house during the winter to engage himself in business affairs in Vienne and Lyons. Flavia was busy also, stalking around the house, looking for ways to make improvements, summoning builders and artists to make plans for extensions and new decorations.

Several times she had slaves whipped for minor infractions and her maid, a tall, slender girl from Spain, limped for a month after a thrown pot of pomade had almost shattered her knee.

Flavia summoned me often in order to check the accounts, far too often than was necessary, having me sit beside her and explain various items. Usually we were alone and, at such times, she would press her knee against me and often, as if by accident, touch my arms and thighs.

One day in spring she said to me, 'Atilus, your skin is very smooth and hard. It's almost like ivory, did you know that?'

'I hadn't thought about it, Domina.'

'And your face. If you wore your hair curled . . . so,' she arranged it, 'you would look like the statue of Apollo on the Palatine.' Without change of tone she asked, 'Have you known a woman?'

I flushed and she smiled at my silence, but thought nothing of the question. A slave had no privacy.

'As you know, your master is a man of the highest moral standard,' she continued. 'Slaves will be selected for sale later in the year. If you don't want to be among them it would be best if you restrained your desires. Do you understand?'

'Yes, Domina.'

'I hope that you do. Now let us check these figures again.' She leaned over the scroll, tapping it with her polished nail. 'There seems to be a discrepancy in the amount of wine and I think you may have added this column incorrectly.'

Chilo shook his head at me when, after one such episode, I returned to the office. He had been drinking and the air was heavy with fumes of wine from his breath.

'I warned you, Atilus.'

'About what?'

'Making up to Flavia.'

'I'm not, but I can't refuse to obey her when she sends for me.'

'Who said that you could? But there's a way of looking at a woman. A hint given with the eyes. A compliment paid without words. Don't do it. From what I see you're comfortable here, good food, wine, plenty of girls willing to warm your bed if you give them the word. You should pick one and fill her belly with child.'

Some scrolls lay on the desk. I sorted them and thrust them into their correct holes in the rack. One fell to the floor and, as I stooped to pick it up, Chilo ran his hand up under my tunic and over my buttocks.

I tensed and then, as his fingers began questing, rose and spat in his eyes.

'What—' He recoiled, startled, spittle running down his cheeks.

'Don't touch me!'

'I meant no harm. You don't go with girls so I thought—' He broke off, shrugging. 'All right, so I made a mistake, but where's the harm? A lot of men are like that and, you, looking like a Greek, well, let's just forget it, eh?'

'I'm not a Greek.'

'No, but you've certainly got a temper. The way you looked – who would have guessed it?' He wiped his face with the back of his hand. 'I came to tell you the news. Flavia's talked Severus into backing a spectacle at the local arena.

Officially Gratus is giving it. It'll only be a small display, but anything's better than nothing, and a day's show should get him all the votes he needs.'

'Gladiators in the arena?'

'That's right.' Chilo grinned. 'The day after tomorrow. If you've got a little money I could maybe double it with a few bets.'

CHAPTER 5

Severus was absent and sent word that, because of an unavoidable delay, he would not be able to return until the day after the munera. Flavia, trembling with anger, crushed the scrap of parchment in her hands. Gratus tried to soothe her.

'It doesn't matter, Flavia. Everything is arranged. I don't need him.'

'You don't need him, but what about me?' She stormed at his expression. 'Am I to stay at home and miss the entertainment my husband has paid for? You, as editor, will be busy. Macer is away. Am I to go alone like a common woman and be fondled by any man who takes a fancy to what he sees?'

'Don't exaggerate, Flavia.'

'It happens, Gratus. Severus has a position to uphold and it would be undignified for me to go unattended.

Gratus frowned. He'd drunk too much wine the evening before and his wits were slow. Then, glancing at me, he smiled.

'Take, Atilus.'

'Atilus?'

'Why not? It's the custom in Rome and, if tongues wag, Severus has only himself to blame.'

We left early, Gratus with Chilo riding ahead as I trotted beside Flavia's litter. The bearers were strained to the utmost, sweat running down their faces, chests heaving as we neared the town. A short rest and we pushed our way through the narrow streets.

The amphitheatre was at the far side away from the river, the builders taking advantage of a natural hollow. It was made of wood, the tiers steeply ranked about the actual arena which was an oval covered with sand about a hundred feet long by seventy wide. The surrounding wall was about twelve feet high and its rim edged the first tier. It was pierced with openings; there were the two portals of Life and Death of course, and others through which slaves and animals would be thrust.

The Master of Games, a fat and balding man, bowed as he greeted Flavia.

'Madam, this is indeed a pleasure. Your husband?'

'Has been detained.'

'A pity, but his money has been put to good use. I've managed to get some animals and some good gladiators. That is,' he coughed, 'as good as could be obtained with the funds available. Now it would be as well to hurry if you don't want to miss the opening.'

A slave guided her to a seat on the podium and she sat close to Gratus in his position of honour. It was a privilege, but Severus had paid and his wife deserved to be accommodated. Other notables of the town sat on the first tier, behind them the rich merchants and traders, above them the ordinary people. Every seat was taken, men mixed with women in the local fashion. Hawkers moved along the aisles offering drinks, sweetmeats of honeyed nuts dusted with spice, small cakes and dried fruits.

It was still fairly early in the year and the awnings had not been raised, but the mass of spectators had brought fans in case the sun should prove too hot. I used one as I stood behind Flavia, creating a gentle wind, a breeze not strong enough to disturb her hair.

Trumpets sounded and heralds announced Gratus as the holder of the games. He rose, smiling at the cheers, confident that, if the crowd liked the show, he was as good as elected.

Sitting down he raised his hand, held it poised for a moment, then brought it sharply down.

The procession began.

I had heard of the arena and knew of the Romans' love of the ludi, the games, but I had never seen a munera before. First came the acrobats, tumbling, rolling over the sand to take dancing steps, to climb one on the other, to fall and tumble again. They were followed by others but the main spectacle was provided by the actual gladiators themselves.

They marched as if they were soldiers, helmets crested high with nodding plumes, armour bright in the sunlight. Music came from a small orchestra, providing an accompaniment to the regular tread of their feet. They circled the arena, halting to face the empty space reserved for the Emperor, lifted their right arms in the traditional salute.

'Hail, Caesar! We who are about to die salute you!'

The trumpets sounded again and the arena cleared.

Chilo had moved from Gratus's side to where I stood. 'Like it, Atilus?'

'So far.'

'It gets better later on. I've had a word with the Master of Games and those Samnites know what to expect if they put up a poor show.'

'Samnites?'

'The gladiators. That's the old name for them.' Chilo was impatient at my ignorance. 'You know, at a time like this, I wish I was back among them. A soft life has its advantages, but there's something in the roar of the crowd which stirs the blood. You wait, you'll see!'

He moved back to his place as the acrobats came running over the sand. They were skilful, forming human pyramids, doing back-springs, leaping and rolling in their brightly coloured clothing. They were replaced by a bunch of cripples and disfigured men, many old, who carried wooden shields and who beat at each other with whips and staves. The crowd roared at their antics for many of them were truly comical. After this came other men, real gladiators this time using wooden swords. These lusorii were beginners, some the sons of officials trying out their hands against the professionals. They fought until the crowd began to grow a little restless, a change of mood sensed by the Master of Games who ordered the trumpets to be sounded again.

In the interval I served Flavia with wine from a jug I had carried in a basket together with some small freshly baked cakes.

After the interval the gladiators entered the arena again to have the sharpness of their weapons checked by Gratus and the real entertainment of the day began.

The prisons had yielded a handful of condemned criminals and there were some broken slaves, men and women past useful service, some who had proved intractable. They were shoved into the arena as trinqui, sacrificial victims who had no hope of defence or reprieve. Swords had been given to some of the men who were ordered to fight.

I watched as they feebly struck at each other, slaves lashing them on, others searing their flesh with red-hot irons. One cried out as a sword bit into his shoulder and covered him with blood. Another lost a hand and ran in circles, the stump lifted, a ruby stream fountaining from the wound. A third, blinded by a slash across the eyes, groped blindly, his face a mask of blood.

The crowd roared.

It was a sound I had never heard before, a savage, bestial yell as men and women craned forward, mouths open, eyes wide as they revelled in the sight of blood and pain. It rose louder as animals entered the arena, and the attendant slaves ran for their lives, while the now disarmed victims floundered away from the bears and dogs which had been turned against them. They fell beneath claw and fang, throats torn open, stomachs ripped, arms and legs crunched and broken. One man ran to just below where we watched and tried to climb to the podium. Flavia laughed as he fell short, to rise and try again, only to be caught in mid-air with the swipe of a paw which peeled flesh from his back and broke his spine.

The bears had entered first, the dogs following when they had killed most of the trinqui. They beat at the starved hounds as, baited, they stood man-like on the sand. Fur turned red, the blood running in streams, the entire arena covered with dead and dying men and animals.

It was a sight I had hoped never to see again. Suddenly I was a boy once more, standing on the slope beyond the stronghold, watching other men fight and die. The red of blood-matted fur became the cloaks of the legionaries, their claws the flash of swords, their victims the bodies of my own people . . .

'Atilus!'

I blinked and drew a deep breath. My face was moist with sweat and my hands trembled.

'Atilus, that is twice I have spoken to you.' Flavia was looking up at me, her face too was damp with perspiration. 'Fan me!'

I obeyed, looking down into the arena. The event was over, slaves running among the litter of beasts and victims, killing those who were still alive, dragging the bodies through one of the openings with the aid of hooks attached to ropes. More slaves cleaned the arena, smoothing the sand with rakes, covering the blood and mess.

On the podium braziers fumed with incense burned to provide a sweetish scent.

The day passed, there were more animals, bears and lions which were killed by bestiarii, men trained to kill the most savage creatures. One had his scalp torn from his head and another was badly bitten by a lion. These men were slow in action, waiting until they could come to grips with the animals, a reluctance which didn't please the crowd.

Chilo snorted his contempt.

'That's what you get when the money's tight – rubbish! If the Samnites can't do better I'll go down among them myself!'

He meant it. His face was suffused, his eyes bloodshot and his hands quivered as if they held sword and shield. He, Flavia, the entire crowd was intoxicated with the sight of blood.

The gladiators were the high point of the occasion. A hush fell as the first pair entered. The Master of Games was stretching things as far as he could and the smallness of the arena helped. Mass combats used up men fast, but were liked because they provided a better view.

He'd chosen to start with a pair of myrmillones who wore the old armour of Gaul and fought with the sword. They had large shields and helmets adorned with the image of a fish. Their right arms were protected to the shoulder and each man wore a greave on his left shin. Burly, strongly built, they hammered at each other, urged on by their trainers, and lashed when they showed signs of reluctance by slaves wielding heavy straps.

Unable to restrain himself Chilo yelled from where he stood beside Gratus.

'Get in there! Stop beating each other's shields! Show us some blood!'

The demand was taken up and repeated by the crowd which threw scraps of food at the fighters in a display of impatient contempt.

Sensing the mood the gladiators stopped playing around and soon one was on his back, blood on his leg, his shield thrown aside, the forefinger of his right hand raised in a plea for mercy.

Gratus hesitated for only a moment. As the crowd, jeering, signalled their wishes he extended his right hand, the thumb jabbing downwards.

Death!

The victor lowered his uplifted sword and cut at the fallen man's neck. Blood spurted, some of it staining his legs. A man dressed as Charon came running, others clothed as Mercury following close behind. He stooped over the recumbent figure, found signs of life and, removing the helmet, smashed in the temple with a short hammer which he took from his belt. Raising it he displayed the head smeared with blood and brains as the others dragged the body through the Porta Libidiensis – the Gate of Death.

Some pugiles came next, naked apart from loin cloths, their arms and torsos bulging with muscle. They fought with leather bands wrapped around their hands and fitted with spikes. They were clever, weaving and dodging, blocking each other's blows, but soon both were covered with blood from wounds on their arms and shoulders. As one staggered back, half-stunned and blinded from a blow which ripped the flesh above one eye, Flavia gripped my hand and pressed it against her breast.

I felt the soft mound of flesh, the hardness of the nipple and, looking down, could see her face, flushed, the lips moist and parted to reveal her small, white teeth.

She wasn't alone in her excitement. To one side on the second tier a woman cried out as she stood, face strained, eyes glittering, her body moving as she thrust it against the hand questing beneath her garments. And there were other men and women sexually stimulated by the sight of blood.

The bout ended, the loser being granted mercy by the crowd which fluttered handkerchiefs. Gratus was eager to please them and held up his thumb.

'Atilus!' Flavia pressed my hand harder against her body. 'Isn't it exciting?'

'Yes, Domina.' The sight had sickened me. Looking up I saw Chilo staring at me, caught the quick shake of his head. 'Some wine?'

'No, I—' She broke off, drawing a deep breath. Releasing her grip on my hand she pushed it aside. 'That is, yes, a little. And take some yourself.'

I was grateful for the invitation. The sun had passed the zenith and the heat had parched my tongue. As slaves again cleared the arena I served her in a crystal goblet and took my own wine from a bowl. It went almost at once to my head so that I stood, a little dizzy, waiting for the next event to take place.

It was in the nature of comic relief.

A pair of andabatae, men who fought naked and blind, armed with swords, their heads locked in opaque, enclosing helmets. Slaves guided them into the centre of the arena and thrust them towards each other with forked poles. Unable to see they could only slash wildly at the air, guided by the yelled instructions of the crowd.

'To your left! No, to your right! Move forward! Watch out!'

One was an old man, hair white on his chest, his legs knotted with veins, his paunch sagging. The other was little more than a boy, slim, his body like that of an immature girl. One foot was deformed so that he limped over the sand.

Their swords met, metal clashing, and each began desperately to slash at where they thought the other could be standing. The boy took a cut on the left shoulder and then, turning, another across his buttocks which had the crowd roaring with laughter. The laughter grew as he swept up his blade, the tip slitting the other's paunch so that intestines bulged through the opening like a mass of greasy ropes.

'In, boy, in!'

The old man backed as he heard the yell, his left hand gripping the wound, blood dribbling over his fingers. Again the swords met, parted to chop down as one, the old man's blade biting deep into a shoulder, that of the boy cutting an arm to the bone.

'Atilus!' Flavia was laughing, tears of amusement in her eyes. 'More wine!'

I poured, the red wine the blood of my mother, my people, aware now as never before of the cruelty of Rome. Slavery, as Didius had said, was common to all nations, the price paid for defeat, but this butchery was something I couldn't understand. Fighting between matched opponents, yes, there could be merit in a test of skill, but wanton, savage killing was pointless.

The bout ended, both men crawling, dying in the sand. The charonian came out to finish them both and the display went on.

CHAPTER 6

It was dusk by the time we got back to the villa, slaves ran with steaming buckets of water to fill Flavia's bath and I grabbed one, taking it among the trees to strip and wash. My body was dirty with sweat and dust. My hair, too, was grimed and I scrubbed it, combing it when it dried. It was more than a matter of hygiene; a house-slave had to be clean and tidy at all times so as not to offend the eyes and nostrils of his owners.

Late that night Flavia sent for me.

I'd been given Didius's old chamber and was lying, restless, dreaming of the arena when a touch on my shoulder brought me awake and sitting upright. Flavia's maid stood beside me, a small lamp in her hand.

'Atilus!'

'What is it?' I frowned at her answer. 'The accounts? Now?'

She shrugged at my expression. In the dim light of the lamp her eyes held a glint of cynical amusement.

'That's what she said, and you are to hurry.' Pausing she added, 'She waits in her bedroom.'

Flavia had decorated the chamber, softening the Spartan simplicity which Severus had preferred with busts, vases, statuettes fashioned in the Grecian style. Rich fabrics carpeted the floor and the wide bed was covered with fine cotton embroidered with patterns in coloured thread. The light was softly yellow from lamps placed at various points, the oil scented, the wicks neatly trimmed.

In their light Flavia looked both young and beautiful. She wore a loose robe of fine linen closed with a wide ribbon at the waist. Beneath its hem I could see the gleam of her naked feet. Her hair had been combed, arranged in a mass of curls, the locks heavily perfumed.

'The accounts, Domina.'

'Put them down.' She moved to a table of inlaid woods and poured wine from a crystal flask. 'I couldn't sleep, Atilus. Today reminded me of the old times in Rome when we used to go to the Circus Maximus. My family backed the green faction. The chariots—' She broke off, looking at me, then shrugged. 'You wouldn't understand. Locked away in the country like this how could you know what life is really like? Even I had almost forgotten. Today reminded me of what I've been missing.'

'The munera?'

'Yes.' She stepped closer to where I stood, sipping her wine. Her face was flushed, her eyes bright, her lips pouted and moist. 'Do you know why we have them, Atilus? It is a part of our tradition. Battle strengthens a man and, once accustomed to the sight of blood, he won't turn weak in times of war. Rome was built on blood and, by blood, it will survive.' Pausing she said, oddly, 'Macer told me that you want to become a soldier.'

I bowed, startled by the change of subject.

'You are a valuable slave, Atilus. Severus will miss you.'

I said nothing, wondering if she knew that he had given me to his son.

'To become a legionary,' she murmured. 'What a waste. You could do better for yourself than that if you had the right patron. Do you really want to join the army?'

'Domina?'

'A hard life with little reward. Severus is old and, perhaps, things will change soon. Life in Rome can be so much more exciting than it is here. A man like you could do well, rich women, rich gifts, a life of comfort and ease instead of the hard discipline of a camp.' She finished her wine and threw me the empty goblet. 'Think about it, Atilus.'

An order which I obeyed as I put the goblet back on the table. There had been a hidden meaning in her words, an unspoken promise, but it would be a mistake to read too much into what she had said. She could be toying with me, testing me, even displaying some of the sadistic nature which Chilo had hinted she possessed.

I wanted to get away from her, to get back to my chamber, to waste the time until Macer should keep his promise. But, until I was freed, I had no choice but to obey.

'Atilus!' Her eyes held mine as I turned to face her. 'Atilus, are you deformed?'

'No, Domina.'

'I must be certain. Strip.'

'Domina?'

'Can't you understand Latin? I gave you an order – obey!' She added, as I stared at her in numbed disbelief, 'I must be sure that you are not disfigured in some way. If you are then you will be placed among the other slaves to be offered for sale.'

'But, Domina, Macer—'

'Owns you, I know. That means nothing. A Roman father owns everything that his children possess. Macer holds you only as long as it suits Severus to allow him to do so. He could take you and everything else the boy has and leave him destitute if he wished. And I, Atilus, have great influence with Severus. Now strip and let me see you naked.'

The threat was plain, obey her or she would ruin my chance of freedom. The Patria Potestas gave Severus the right to do as she said, he could sell me before Macer returned from Rome. A father was to his son as an owner was to his slave.

'Atilus!'

My single garment fell to the floor, the lamplight glowing on my skin as, naked, I turned for her inspection.

'Beautiful!' She came closer to me, breathing quickly.

'Atilus, your body is beautiful.' Her hands glided over my chest, my belly, my loins. Overwhelmed by her nearness, her femininity, I could not help but react. 'Atilus!'

She stepped back, hands going to her waist, the robe opening as she pulled at the ribbon. Beneath it she was naked. I looked at the mounds of her breasts tipped with prominent nipples, the curve of her stomach, her thighs. Her skin glowed with a nacrous sheen in the soft, yellow light.

'Take me, Atilus,' she whispered. 'Take me.'

'Severus—'

'Is away. We are safe. Now take me, quickly now! Take me!'

The robe fell from her shoulders as she closed the gap between us, pressing her body against mine, softness coupled with a demanding heat. The cover rumpled as I lifted her and placed her on the bed, all caution lost in the fury of my own passion. She gasped as I mounted her, sighed as she felt the gush of my emission. A prelude, I was young, impulsive, long-restrained desire bursting free.

She writhed as I moved within her body, head turning from side to side, her nails raking my shoulders, my back. Her teeth met in my shoulder as she reached her climax and she fell back blood on her mouth, more dripping on her breasts from the shallow wound.

'Atilus, my darling,' she murmured. 'My wonderful lover. My gladiator. Stab me again, darling. Again!'

It was easy to obey. She was nothing like Celia had been, she used arts the simple girl hadn't known, moving herself against me, arousing me with her heat, inflaming passion into a bursting demand. Young, virile, I was a rutting animal feeding a hunger long denied. There came a time of madness in which I lost myself, conscious of nothing but the woman beneath me, her nearness, her softness, her demands.

And, when cooled, I looked down at her, there was no ghost from the past. Only a woman with swollen lips and a ruby mouth, lips stained with the blood which dappled her breasts and smeared my shoulder and chest.

She rubbed her hand over it, licked it with her tongue.

'My gladiator,' she whispered. 'My man.'

I caressed her, her hand guiding my own, a little afraid now as I wondered what was to happen. It was as if she could read my thoughts.

'You must be discrete, Atilus. If you talk I shall know and will deny anything you may say. You will be whipped and sold to the galleys.'

'But your maid?'

'Will say nothing if she knows what is good for her.'

She had accompanied Flavia from Rome and I remembered the glint of amusement in her eyes. To her such incidents must be common.

'There will be other occasions,' whispered Flavia. 'But you must never mark my body. Severus is uncivilised in such matters, but he is old and cannot give me what I need.'

'And me, Domina?'

'There will be small gifts and, later, when we are in Rome—' My caresses had aroused her. 'Atilus!'

This time the fires were slower to erupt, her pleasure the greater because of it. She moaned a little, making odd, animal-like cries which drowned all outer sounds so that I didn't hear the footsteps and knew nothing of Severus's arrival until he entered the room.

The sight must have stunned him.

'Flavia! What—'

She cried out and pushed me away, a simple task for I was already rising.

'Rape!' she gasped. 'He came and I couldn't stop him. He—'

I glanced at her, bewildered as she broke into a storm of weeping. Severus made a choking sound and ran towards me. He had doffed his cloak but still wore the belt and sword he'd carried on his journey. The blade flashed as he drew it and swung it towards my face.

Ducking I felt the wind as it passed over my head.

'Master!'

He turned, snarling, and I caught his wrist as the blade came close. For a moment we strained and I could feel his stringy muscles, the thin flesh over his brittle bones. He glared like a madman, his lips blue, eyes bulging from their sockets. Foam edged his mouth and then, as with maniacal strength he tore himself free, he stumbled and fell to strike his head against a table.

'Atilus!' Flavia stared at me from the bed. 'Is he dead?'

I stooped over the limp figure. Blood showed on a minor cut on the temple but, though unconscious, Severus was alive.

'No.'

'Then kill him.' Her voice rose, harsh with impatience. 'Hurry, you fool. Kill him before it's too late!'

Before he recovered and sent me to the galleys for having raped his wife. Flavia's demand made sense.

'Hurry!' She threw me a pillow. 'Hold it hard over his face.'

Once Severus was dead she would be a widow again and rich enough to enjoy life in Rome. She might denounce me, but it was a chance I had to take.

'Hurry!'

A slave is accustomed to obey. Holding the pillow I knelt at the fallen man's side, turning him over so that he lay on his back. Severus was old, it would take only minutes to end his life. He stirred, eyelids fluttering as I moved the pillow towards his mouth.

Chilo grabbed me from behind.

He had entered with Gratus and was far from gentle. He lifted me as if I'd been a child, his voice a rasp in my ear.

'Fool! Kill him and we'd all be executed! Every slave in the house!'

He slammed me against a wall, stooping to snatch up the sword, holding it with the point inches from my naked body. No longer the casual drunkard he looked hard, dangerous, poised on his feet with practiced grace.

Gratus looked at me, at Flavia, at Severus moving feebly on the floor.

'It seems we arrived in good time,' he said. 'What happened?'

'Atilus raped me. He came into the room while I was getting ready for bed and—'

'You struggled and screamed and were over-powered,' Gratus interrupted. 'Yes, sister, I understand. A pity that your husband returned too soon.'

'You doubt me?'

'What I think isn't important,' he said dryly. 'Severus is the man you have to convince.'

He was moving, sitting upright and holding his head. Gratus went to him, helped him to a chair, gave him wine.

'Flavia?'

'I'm all right, darling.' She had put on her robe and crossed to him, gently bathing his temple. 'Thank the gods you arrived in time!'

'An appointment cancelled,' he muttered. 'I'd hoped to have arrived earlier.' He seemed dazed. Gratus gave him more wine.

'Drink this,' he urged. 'It will help.'

Severus pushed aside the goblet. His wits were clearing, his memory returning.

'Flavia! You and that slave!'

'I couldn't help it! Severus, do you think I invited him here?' She pulled open her robe, showed him the scratches on her shoulders, the blood smeared on her breasts. 'And look!' More scratches were on her thighs, the skin torn by her own nails when attention had been concentrated on Severus. 'He came in here like an animal. I couldn't resist him.'

'Why didn't you scream?'

'He had his hand over my mouth.' The swollen lips stained with the blood she had licked were proof of her claim.

'No!' I said sharply. 'It wasn't like that! She sent for me to check the accounts!'

'That was the excuse he gave when he came,' she said quickly. 'Some figures he asked me to check. See? The rolls are there. I looked at them and, when I turned, he was naked. Then—' She broke off, dabbing at her eyes. 'Severus, it was horrible! I thought he would kill me. He would have killed me if you hadn't arrived when you did.'

This time Severus took the wine Gratus offered him. His hands were trembling so that he had to clutch the goblet with both of them, wine spilling as he lifted it to his mouth.

'Atilus,' he said thickly. 'He tried to kill me.'

'No, master!' I stepped forward, halted at the prick of the sword. 'We struggled, don't you remember? You tried to cut me and I held your wrist. Then you fell. I was putting a pillow beneath your head when the others came.'

Chilo rumbled, 'That's right, Domini. That's what he was doing when we arrived.'

Gratus said nothing, but watched, his eyes cynical, and I sensed that he regretted his early arrival. Had he delayed a while longer in the town it would all have been over by now.

'Severus!' Flavia dropped to her knees beside him. 'You must believe me. It happened just the way I said. I can't bear to talk about it. Your own wife, attacked by a slave, I must kill myself to wipe out the disgrace!'

For a moment I thought he would agree and ten years earlier, perhaps, he would have done, but he was old and Flavia looked very young and lovely as she crouched at his feet.

'No,' he said. 'No.'

'But the disgrace?'

'Will have to be faced.'

'Why?' said Gratus calmly. 'Need anyone know? Fortunately the house has not been aroused and we can keep this to ourselves. A quiet disposal, Severus, it is the better way.'

'He must die!'

'True, but there is more than one way of dealing death. If he is to be condemned then evidence will have to be given and rumour will spread the story. Macer could hear of it in Rome. Chilo could have an accident with that sword, of course, but why be so gentle.'

'The galleys—'

'A long journey and they pay little. I've a better suggestion. Let me sell him to the arena. Not here, of course, but I know a lanista who will take him to another region. He could be used as one of the trinqui.'

To be thrown to the beasts, to be torn apart, to die listening to the shrieks of the crowd as they revelled in my pain.

'Master, no! I am innocent!'

He wasn't listening, the evidence was against me, nothing would change his mind.

I was eighteen years old.

CHAPTER 7

Once again I marched through Gaul as a captive slave. Quintus Plotius, the lanista, was a tall, lean man with a hare lip and an infection on his hands which caused the skin to crack and weep. He had brought his familia to Vienne and the troop of gladiators kept rough time as they swung down the road towards Italy.

When buying me he had said little, studying me through the grill set into the door of the cabin in which I had been held waiting his arrival.

Chilo, sneaking me scraps of meat to augment the bread and water I had been given, had been roughly comforting.

'You were a fool, Atilus. Why didn't you listen when I tried to warn you?'

'I couldn't disobey.'

'You could have pleaded that you were sick. Had a stomach ache or something. A finger down your throat would have made you vomit. No woman wants to go to bed with a retching slave.'

Good advice which had come too late.

'Gratus knows,' continued Chilo, 'but what could he have done? Severus wanted revenge.' Pausing he added, casually, 'That pillow? Her idea?'

'I was—'

'Going to kill him, that was obvious. If he'd guessed that nothing could have saved you. The woman's idea?'

'Yes.'

'I thought so. She's a real bitch. Well, it's happened, Atilus, and you'll have to live with it. Now take some good advice. Hold your head high, walk proud, act the man. I know Plotius and he won't throw good material to the beasts no matter what he's promised. I'll have a word with him, but it's up to you.' He stared at me through the grill. 'Good luck, Atilus – you'll need it.'

Marching in the column I could believe it. Escape was impossible, my hands were lashed behind me and my feet hobbled. I could walk but if I tried to run I would fall. One of the other captives had tried it and had been whipped until his back ran red with blood.

The gladiators had looked on, stolidly indifferent to his pain.

They were hard men, many wounded, bandages covering ugly wounds. The pugile I had seen lose in the arena was one of the worst, his scalp had been torn and roughly sewed, the jagged rip swollen and crusted with oozing pus. He left it bare so as to receive the sunlight, a thing he swore would aid the healing.

'A Jew told me about it,' he said one night as he sat staring into the fire. 'A physician from Tarsus. I met him at a munera held at Pompeii. I was with Marcellus Junius – any of you know him?'

A secutor spat in the fire.

'I know him. A wolf. All he wants is money and he doesn't care how he gets it.'

'That's him.'

'I travelled with him for a while and almost got myself killed. We'd fixed a deal with a retiarius, I was to go down under his net and the editor would give the thumbs up. If he didn't the retiarius was to fake the death blow. The charonian had been bribed so there was nothing to worry about. The worst that could happen was I'd get hurt a little. Well, the crowd was against me and I can't really blame them. I'd drunk too much the night before and was slow, missing chances and staying too clear for their liking. Anyway, to cut it short, I dropped as arranged and signalled for mercy. The editor saw the crowd was against me and the bastard rode along with them. I still wasn't worried and then I saw the retiarius's eyes. He was from Spain.'

'Slimy types,' said one of the others. 'You can't trust them.'

'So I found out. He didn't intend to play along. I rolled as the trident came down, grabbed his legs, threw him and opened his guts with his own dagger. The crowd loved it.'

'And Junius?'

'I left him – once was enough. Say what you like about Quintus, he plays fair.'

So the talk went on. Remembering Chilo's advice I'd thrust myself among them as they sat at the fire at night. At first they'd pushed me away, professionals not wanting the company of a slave, but I'd persisted and finally they gave in. I'd helped in other ways, too, bathing wounds and serving the bowls of cooked barley and meat. Quintus Plotius had freed my hands at such times in order to use my labour.

And, listening, I learned.

Not all gladiators were slaves, in fact only three of those in Plotius's familia were not free and two of those had been hired out to him by their owners. The rest were freedmen or citizens who had deliberately chosen the arena as their profession. They travelled widely in the pursuits of their careers, hiring themselves to various lanistae, grumbling at times because of the lack of work. A lanista wasn't essential, but the man acted as manager and took care of details so that most of them preferred to act under their direction. One of them, Nonius, an ex-slave, had won the rudis, the symbolical wooden sword which had given him his freedom.

Nonius had come from Sicily, a dark, swarthy man, with liquid eyes and a badly scarred torso.

He was of the group of gladiators known as Thracians, fighting with an open helmet, a small, round shield and the curved blade, the sica. Apart from his right arm and left shin his body was unprotected, he fought naked but for a belt from which hung an apron to cover his genitals. He told us how he'd won his freedom one night after the meal when stars had begun to glimmer in the heavens.

'It was at Perugia and we were celebrating the Emperor's marriage to Agrippinilla. That was, let me see now, about two years ago. Anyone here ever seen Claudius?'

'I did once,' grunted Magnus. He was the pugile who had won. 'At the Circus. A small man with a big head and weak legs. Drunk most of the time.' Shrugging he added, 'With a wife like that who can blame him?'

'Nags?'

'All the time. That bitch wants to rule Rome and will if given half a chance. She's got a boy, Nero, and once Claudius is out of the way she'll run him like a puppet on a string.'

'Unless Britannicus is made Emperor,' said another. 'The senate might choose him as the natural heir.'

'Which means nothing.' Magnus glowered at the fire. 'The Praetorians are the ones who decide just as they did after assassinating Caius Caligula; they found Claudius hiding in a cupboard when they raided the palace. He was scared and promised them a bonus if they would spare his life. They did more than that, they lifted him up on their shields and proclaimed him Emperor.'

'He hasn't been so bad. He did win us Britain.'

'Us? Those parasites who hang around him, you mean.' Umbricus was a myrmillo, a dour man who rarely spoke, but who had a good reputation for savagery in the arena. 'What did we get out of it? I had to lower my fee because of the glut of slaves. Eight thousand of them after the conquest and more coming all the time. They cheapen the market and make it hard for a man to earn a decent living.'

'Atilus is a Briton,' said the secutor. His voice was suggestive, sly.

'Well? Doesn't that prove what I say?' Umbricus glowered at the fire. 'If we had any sense we'd cut his throat before he can stand against us. I'm fed up with risking my neck against cheap labour. If you win you gain nothing, if you lose the crowd turns against you. Some good men have been lost that way.'

There was a mutter of agreement and I felt the skin prickle between my shoulders. Men with a grievance, imagined or not, made dangerous companions.

'Some more broth, Umbricus?'

'What?' He scowled at me then, suddenly, laughed. It was like the bark of a dog, but it eased the tension. 'You've got guts, boy, I'll give you that. Don't worry, you can sleep safe. Right, lads?' He nodded as they agreed. 'Good. Now let's hear the rest of your story, Nonius.'

He told it well and, in imagination, I could feel the heat of the sun, the rasp of the sand beneath my feet, sense the anticipation of the crowd.

'Claudius wanted to put on a show and didn't spare the expense. I'll skip the preliminaries, you all know what they are, but he did have one novelty. A score of girls dressed as Diana and armed with bows set against as many African pygmies armed with long spears. The girls won, of course, only losing a few of their number before shooting the pygmies down, but then lions were turned against them. They hadn't expected that and when the crowd saw their expressions they let out a laugh which could be heard for miles.'

'A nice touch,' said Magnus. 'Then what happened?'

'I was in the next event; five pairs, to the death and no messing about. All Thracians and, believe me, you could have heard a pin drop as we faced each other. I'd drawn a Syrian and he came at me like lightning. For a while it was all cut and parry then I felt his blade slice over my shoulder as I dropped to cut at his leg. I was lucky and caught him just back of the knee and he was crippled and knew it. I played him safe for a while, letting him bleed and keeping him on the move so as to wear him down, but I couldn't hold back too long. They had a full programme and time was limited. Anyway I took a chance and went in. He slashed my back but I got him down and, naturally, Claudius gave him the thumbs down.'

'So?' The secutor frowned. 'Nothing special in that.'

'No, but that wasn't the end of it. I opened his throat and was taking a bow when one of the others rushed at me. I guess he was the Syrian's lover and he damned near chopped my spine. If it hadn't been for the yell of the crowd he'd have got me for sure. As it was I turned just in time, blocked the cut and managed to get in one of my own on his shield arm. I was pretty wild, dirty play like that gets me, and I went in seeing red.'

'I know how it is,' said Umbricus. 'Back-stabbers like that get me the same way.'

'Yes, well, I was lucky. He couldn't use his shield so it was easy meat. I concentrated on his sword-arm and got in an upward slash which almost took it right off. If the sica hadn't been blunt by that time I'd have cut through bone and armour both. As it was he went running around with his arm flapping and blood spraying all over. The crowd loved it and Claudius was rolling in his seat. That's when he gave me the rudis.'

'And your freedom?'

'Sure.' Nonius looked at me. 'One goes with the other. I got a silver bowl too filled with money. And there was a woman, a patrician – but that's another story.'

'An old one.' The secutor leered. 'We've all had our moments.'

He was ready to talk of amorous exploits, but I gave him no chance.

'You got your freedom,' I said. 'But you still fight in the arena?'

'Why not?' Nonius shrugged. 'I thought of buying a wine shop, but the money went and, well, I began to miss the life.

So I hired out to Quintus and have been travelling around ever since.'

'Talking about women,' said the secutor. 'Did I ever tell you about the wife of a senator who took a fancy to me? It was in Rome and she ...'

I moved back from the circle, thoughtful. One chance at freedom had been lost, Macer couldn't help me now, but another seemed to have offered itself. If I, too, could win the rudis then I, too, would be free.

Sleep was slow in coming that night. The bonds replaced on my hands, lashed before me now with a thong attached to my feet, chafed and made it difficult to adopt a comfortable position, but they were not the reason. For the first time since leaving the villa I had hope.

The hope grew as the days passed. Several times I noticed Quintus Plotius stare at me as, following Chilo's advice, I walked straight with shoulders thrown back, a contrast to the other slaves he had bought who shuffled along with their eyes fixed to the road. From time to time the road-guard would pass us, riding straight on their mounts, the tips of their lances bright in the sun.

Once a party of them halted to question the lanista.

'Where to?'

'Cuneo.'

'From?'

'Vienne. Why, officer, trouble?'

'Nothing serious. We found a dead man in the road a few miles along. Stabbed and robbed, but I guess your gladiators will provide enough protection. Just keep watchful at night.'

'I will. We should make Celer's inn before dark.'

It was a low rambling house with a courtyard attached into a corner of which I and the other captives were herded. Celer, the owner, was a squat, bristling man who had lost his right hand. He had a slattern of a wife, her hair hanging lank and greasy over her dirty face, the loose mounds of her breasts hanging low under a soiled gown. Her voice was grating like the rasp of a nail over slate.

'Celer, we want no gladiators here! They'll give the place a bad name. I've not sweated for years so that you can entertain your friends.'

'They can pay.'

'Bad money. Everyone knows the bustuarii are unlucky.'

Bustuarii – funeral men, an old name for gladiators and a relic of the past when they had fought over the graves of the dead as part of the burial customs.

The argument raged, dying as Celer, goaded beyond endurance, fetched her a slap across the mouth. Later, sitting with Quintus in the common room, he mourned his fate.

'If I hadn't lost a hand I wouldn't be here now. That bitch gets worse every day. Just because a trader stayed here last week she thinks I can afford to turn away custom. When I think of the old days!' He sighed and called for more wine. A girl, little more than a child, served it, lingering to stare at me as I stood against a wall. Quintus, for reasons of his own, had fetched me inside.

'What do you think of him, Celer?'

The man glanced at me. 'Cheap?'

'Cheap enough.'

'Then what can you lose?' The man gulped at his wine. 'Anything's good enough to throw to the beasts.'

'True, but I'd like your opinion.'

A lie, Quintus didn't need it, but I guessed that he was being politic, appealing to the other so as to enhance his dignity for the sake of good relations. I stiffened as Celer rose and came towards me, prodding me with his hand.

'Well built, but soft. A house slave?'

'Yes. He came from Britain, his father was a Gaul.'

'A German I'd say, or someone fathered by one from the

colour of his hair. What did he do, ride his master's mare?' He grunted at the answer. 'I thought so. It happens all the time. A bored woman, a good-looking slave, what else could you expect?'

'What would you think of his chances?'

'In the arena?' Celer shrugged. 'That depends. He's got the face and body but does he have the spirit? A man's useless on the sand if he hasn't got the guts to fight. Hot irons and straps are all very well, but the crowd likes to see a display of courage. That's the trouble nowadays, the fighters are afraid of getting hurt and the crowd knows it.' He rubbed at his chin, fingers rasping over stubble. 'I don't know, Quintus. He might make out and then again he might not. Taken in Britain you say?'

'At the time of the conquest.'

'Eight years ago – that's a long time. House-life softens them. Tell you what, though, you could use him as a novelty. Dress him up as Hercules and set him against bears or lions. Or as Prometheus chained to a rock with eagles to tear out his guts. It'll be good for a laugh at least.'

His tone was casual, unfeeling, to him I was nothing, a scrap of flesh to be ripped apart for a brief amusement. I smelt the stench of him, the stale sweat, the rancid oil he'd used to ease his sores, the foul breath as he came close. Roman scum – and I was a warrior of the Iceni!'

At least I could die like a man!

My shoulders bulged, the muscles in biceps and arms bunching, the thongs bursting from my wrists as I strained against them in sudden, maniacal fury. Celer backed, his face shocked, afraid as my hands lifted to grip his sleazy throat.

'Atilus!' Quintus had risen. 'Atilus!'

I stumbled as I tried to lunge forward, the thong tying my legs forgotten in my rage. I fell, catching at the edge of the table, knocking it down so that wine spilled from the bowls to drench my face and hair.

‘He’s gone mad! Kill him!’

‘No.’ Quintus grabbed Celer and held him. ‘Did you see his face? Did you?’

‘A beast! He intended to kill me! He would have—’

‘Torn you apart had he been given the chance.’ Quintus carried a dagger, he drew it, lamplight running along the oiled blade as he aimed the point at me. I stared at it, knowing that he would use it if I moved, knew too that even if I broke free there was nowhere I could go. It was a time for cunning.

‘Master, I forgot myself!’ Pride, now, meant death and a useless death at that. ‘I—’

‘His face, Celer, a killer’s if I ever saw one.’

‘So?’

‘He has the face and the body, that you agree, and now I know that he has the guts. Chilo hinted as much but I didn’t believe him. Now I know he spoke the truth.’ Quintus gestured with the dagger. ‘On your feet, Atilus. Save that fury for the arena. When you’re trained you could be the finest investment I’ve ever made.’

CHAPTER 8

The gladiatorial school at Cuneo was built like a stronghold, the walls were high, broken only by a door fitted with metal-studded panels. Beyond it lay a small courtyard and another open area, larger, at the end of a short passage running through facing buildings. I looked around as Quintus Plotius halted us inside. The buildings were of two storeys, the upper rooms opening onto a gallery supported on wooden posts.

The air was full of sound; the clink and rasp of metal, hammering, the shouted orders of instructors from the larger open area where men were busy at exercise. Armed guards stood by the gate, others patrolled the galleries. The place was not a stronghold but a prison, the guards a defence to ease local fears.

The owner was Bracas Murallius, a burly man with hard, narrowed eyes. He came forward to greet Quintus, staring at the captive slaves he had brought with him. The gladiators had gone, running to the baths to wash, later to eat and join their colleagues in the halls flanking the exercise area.

'Quintus!' Bracas extended his hand and they saluted each other, right hand to right wrist. 'Have a good trip?'

'Fair.'

Though a lanista Bracas Murallius didn't travel, leaving that to the other lanistae who used his school as a depot and a source of new material. A commercial arrangement to mutual advantage. Now he looked critically at the slaves.

'Poor stuff, Quintus. You want them trained?'

'Only those that are worth the trouble – I'll sell the rest for use as trinqui. How's business?'

'Good. Alus Antonius is after election and put on a three-day show. Eighty pairs. The duumvir is providing a munera next week, seventy pairs and a score of bestiarii – they'll be coming from Parma. They've skimmed the prisons but we're still short of men so you should get a good price. Want me to handle it?'

Quintus nodded. 'Have you seen Fuscus?'

'No, but I did hear that he ran into bad luck at Firenze and lost over half his familia. I'll tell you about it later, but you could be in trouble, Quintus, I warned you about going into partnership with him.'

'Fuscus is a good man.'

'Honest, yes, but sometimes careless. He gets carried away and over-rates his gladiators. He may have arranged matters so as to make a pile on the betting, but I doubt it. He hasn't got a shrewd enough mind for that.' Bracus shrugged. 'Well, let's see what you've got.'

He moved down the line, jerking up heads with his hand, punching arms and shoulders, feeling thighs. He halted before me, frowning.

'What's this? A pretty boy?'

Quintus explained, adding, 'I want him trained, Bracus, and I don't want him spoiled.'

'Something special?' Bracus's eyes were gimlets as they examined me. 'I can't see it. He looks soft. You could be wasting your money, Quintus. Why not take a quick profit and have done with it?'

Bracus didn't own all his slaves, many of them he trained for a fee, offering the benefits of his school to various lanistae who couldn't afford their own establishment. Dismissing the others he listened to what Quintus had to say, standing beyond earshot, nodding as the conversation ended.

Returning he said, 'So you had a little trouble as a boy, eh? Found the dead body of your mother. Raped, wasn't she? Held down and opened and used. Ever thought of what it must have been like for her? Try to imagine it – knocked down on your back, someone standing on your wrists, others spreading your legs. Then the rest get to work. You ever see a sword penetrate flesh? The tip presses and then digs in, the blood come and wets the blade so it slips in easier. If the sword was a man it would add its own wetness so making it easier for the next to follow. One after the other, each taking turns, a dozen, maybe, even more. Did you love your mother, boy?'

I stared at him through a fog, old memories wakened, old imaginings returned to torment my mind. My mother, held down, forced, raped by Roman swine, murdered to shut her mouth!

'You—'

The flat of his hand lashed across my cheek.

'Think of them, boy! All riding your mother, holding her down, using her time and time again. She'd have screamed and tried to fight. Can you hear her screaming? Can you?'

I spat and lunged forward, suddenly aware of men behind me, of hands gripping me tight.

Again Bracus sent his hand lashing across my face.

'You'd like to kill me, wouldn't you?'

Another blow.

'You'd like to come at me with a sword, cutting, stabbing, seeing the colour of my guts.' Abruptly he said, 'Do you hate Rome?'

'I—' The words were hard to stop, the curses, but just in time sanity prevailed. I was a slave, a potential danger, one which would be eliminated if too threatening. 'No.'

'You're a liar,' he said dispassionately. 'Your face betrayed you. And no one would love those who did all that to your mother. Hate is valuable but it has to be controlled, mastered, used. And I'll give you a warning. Here you obey. If you don't then you'll suffer. If you strike an instructor or rebel in any way you'll be crucified.' He nodded to those holding me. 'Let him go.'

He watched me like a cat as the hands fell away. I was

sweating, trembling, burning with anger, but I knew that, if I yielded to it, I would terminate my life on a cross.

'*Live!*' my mother had told me. '*Live, Atilus, live!*'

Revenge would have to wait.

Bracus grunted as I forced myself to relax. At his side Quintus said, 'Well, wasn't I right?'

'It's early days yet, but I'll take him on. The usual fee and I could be interested in taking a part of him as a personal investment. A half share, maybe?'

'A quarter and you pay for the training.'

They settled on a third and I entered the school at Cuneo.

A slave led me to the baths and then to the dining hall where I was given a bowl of barley mixed with plenty of meat. Gladiators ate a great deal of barley believing that it thickened the arteries and slowed bleeding. So much that we were sometimes called hordearii or barley eaters. We were fed a special kind of ashes after exercise too, a greyish grit washed down with diluted wine. I never knew just what they consisted of, but Togatus, who prepared them, had a contract at the arena for the hearts, livers and genitals of men and beasts. I suspected that he mixed them with spined thorns, prickly pears and other herbs and burned them so as to concentrate their goodness.

After the meal the slave took me to my room. It was on the upper floor, a chamber about eight feet square containing a plank, two blankets, a hollowed wooden block for a head-rest and a row of pegs hammered into a wall on which garments could be hung. A shelf held a pot of water, another pot standing on the floor which was to be used for natural functions during the night when I was to be locked in.

Eperus, the slave, explained it all to me as he stood in the open doorway.

'Bracus is hard but fair. Go along with him and you'll learn, cross him and—' He drew his forefinger over his throat. 'You want some advice, Atilus? Just keep your mouth shut and your ears open. There'll be some horseplay, but take it in good part. I don't mean just lie down under it, but don't be too quick to take offence.'

I looked past him at the other buildings flanking the exercise yard. 'Those?'

He explained that gladiators were divided into three groups, the myrmillones, the retiarii who fought with net and trident, and the Thracians. The groups contained others of various types, for example the myrmillones included the secutors, the dimachaeri who fought with two daggers, were with the Thracians, the retiarii included the laquearii who used lassos instead of a net.

Bestiarii, the animal-fighters, were a different branch of gladiators and were trained in their own schools.

'And this building?'

'For the beginners. You'll be moved later when it's decided what you are to be. That'll be after you're toughened up with work.' Eperus grinned. 'And, Atilus, that means *hard* work.'

At the villa I'd seen the field-slaves labouring from before dawn until dusk on the land. Now I became one of them, working not on the land but in the school. The day began long before dawn when I rose to clean the fires, sweep the galleries, fetch and carry loads of wood and grain. It was brutal labour conducted at the double, stung by the whips of the overseers whenever they came within range. Quickly I learned to dodge the lashes, helped by my previous training with Macer and, after a while, the loads grew lighter, the journeys seemed to become shorter.

Then outside, under guard, to cut wood, swinging an axe until my shoulders ached and my hands became raw with oozing blisters. The blisters turned into callouses, the ache lessened as muscles toned, the good food and exercise giving my skin a healthy sheen. I built walls, heaving masses of stone, working until it became too dark to see then returned to my room, to slump in exhausted slumber, too tired even to dream.

But later came time for thought and an appreciation of the situation facing every lanista who owned a school.

Men, condemned to almost certain death, needed careful handling. To chain them, whip them, treat them as animals was not the best way to develop the ruthless aggression needed if they hoped to survive in the arena. Yet to develop that aggression was to court danger, to feed a fire which could easily burst beyond control.

The shadow of Spartacus was always present.

Eperus told me about him one evening after the meal when we sat in my room. He was a small man with a narrow face and an alert mind, which made him of value to the school. Without proof I was sure that he reported regularly to Bracus as to the state of mind of the slaves, a spy who could catch whispers and smell out incipient rebellion.

'Spartacus,' he said. 'Have you ever heard of him, Atilus?'

'No.'

'He was a gladiator in the school at Capua. That was over a hundred and twenty years ago now, six hundred and eighty after the founding of Rome. He fell in love with a slave-girl, or had a friend killed, I'm not sure as to the details, but he staged a rebellion. They killed the guards with kitchen knives, grabbed their weapons and broke into the armoury for more. They took over the school and then moved to the crater of Vesuvius. More slaves joined them and they formed quite an army. A legion was sent against them but its commander was a fool. He didn't think it worth the trouble to make a proper camp – after all they were only slaves – and the slave army made a night attack and won. More armour and weapons and still more slaves went to join them. A snowball, you might say. Just a handful of gladiators growing like a fire.'

I looked through the door, conscious of his searching eyes.

'And?'

'It makes you think, doesn't it, Atilus? A few dedicated men setting out to gain freedom.'

'If they were dedicated.'

'What?'

'Things happen,' I explained. 'A man could lose his head and start something he wished he hadn't. Once moving he can't stop. After they had beaten the legion, what then?'

'They moved south. I guess Spartacus wanted to get back home, stupid really, he had no real home. And there was trouble in his command, arguments as to the best thing to do. But it was close. If he hadn't tried to run and had headed for Rome he could have taken the city. As it was Grassius cornered him in the south and cut his army to pieces. They crucified six thousand prisoners along the Appian Way.'

He fell silent and I wondered why he had mentioned the subject. A warning? Or was he sounding me out as a possible recruit for another such episode? If so it was a trap which I could easily avoid.

'They couldn't win,' I said.

'Why not? They almost did.'

'Almost.' I shrugged. 'We almost won in Britain. If Cattigern had held fast – but he didn't and now we're a province of Rome. Spartacus almost won – and his men ended on crosses. The only thing which counts is to win.'

His voice was a purr from the shadows. 'And if he had, Atilus, what then?'

'Nothing. He would have taken over and the patricians would have become slaves. In a few years things would have been the same as before. New masters, perhaps, but that's all. But he could never have won. Undisciplined men can never beat trained soldiers. Gladiators are individuals, the legionaries are part of a machine.'

Eperus chuckled. 'You're smart, Atilus. Behind that pretty face of yours lies a brain. Tomorrow you'd better use it.'

'Why?'

'You're running the gauntlet.'

It took place in the morning, a cruel and savage test of stamina and determination. A double line of men faced each other armed with whips and staves. I and a dozen others had to run between them; if we reached the end we would pass, if not we would be discarded from the school and sold to the arena for use against the beasts.

And the men were determined that we shouldn't pass.

They were hard, tough, proud of their profession, cynical when it came to weakness. And it was an opportunity for them to vent their sadism. Baracus stood to one side with guards, as always, in attendance.

'You!' He pointed at a thin man who stood trembling at the head of our line. 'Now! Move!'

A whip sang through the air, the crack of the lash spiteful as it bit into his flesh, a spur to send him racing towards the double line of waiting men. He relied on speed, covering his face and neck with his hands and arms, blinding himself to the out-thrust foot which tripped him and sent him rolling beneath the hail of blows.

Bloodied, staggering, he regained his feet to lurch on, to fall again, to lie screaming as the staves pulped his legs and back, the whips curling to cut at his face and torso. A grinning myrmillo struck at his genitals, laughing as his stave made impact, the shriek of pain echoing from the surrounding walls.

Beside me a man said, huskily, 'By the gods, they're killing him!'

Bracus stopped them in time, having the man dragged from the line and flung into a corner where he cowered, moaning.

'Next!'

The following man made it as did two others. The next fell, a stave catching one eye and tearing it from its socket, blood masking his face as he staggered blindly on to finally fall, twitching beneath the blows. Then it was my turn.

'Next!'

I was moving before the whip could fall, before the word was even out of the lanista's mouth. Speed would help, but I needed more than speed. The first men, I'd noticed, concentrated on wild swipes of their staves, those lower down the line aimed their whips at the legs, further on, when normally a victim had slowed a little, a burly gladiator aimed at the groin, a few men past him was another who liked to trip the runner.

I couldn't avoid getting hurt but I could, at least, use my brain as Eperus had advised.

The important thing was not to fall, therefore watch those trying to trip me. The eyes and genitals were next, a blow on either could spell defeat. One hand covering my loins, then, the other raised to protect my face. The eyes kept clear to watch for danger – the rest was in the lap of the gods.

My sudden start had surprised them, I'd entered the double line before those closest to me could bring their staves into action. A whip lashed my buttocks, another my back, a stave cracked hard against one shoulder.

Blows I couldn't avoid and had to ignore.

Springing into the air I jumped over a stave a man, dropping, tried to thrust between my legs, landing to veer to one side, uplifted hand knocking aside a thrusting length of wood, feeling against the vicious cut of whips. Ahead the burly gladiator, a pugile, had stepped a little forward from the line and faced me, his stave held like a spear aimed at my groin. Unless deflected the tip would hit my hand, slip between my thighs and bring me down.

I veered again, swinging away from him, racing close to the others – too close to give them time to take aimed blows. Even so I was hurt, seeing stars and feeling something wet and warm run over my temple. My uplifted arm felt numb, the flesh bruised, the bone almost broken. I staggered, drooped for a moment, then raced on, gasping as I broke from the far end of the line.

'Atilus!' Water drenched me, thrown from a bucket held by Eperus. 'Listen to them!'

The men were cheering, shouting, laughing as they stared at me. I dabbed at my face, saw blood on my hand, felt more coming from a cut on my scalp. My buttocks stung and, turning, I saw the reason for the laughter. A stave had caught my garment, ripping it open from waist to hem, exposing the naked flesh beneath.

'Look at those cheeks!' yelled a man. 'Soft to the hand, eh, lads?'

'Better than a woman, Pugnax – but I saw him first!'

'Wait your turn, Decimus!'

Eperus saw my expression. 'Smile, you fool! They're only joking. Smile!'

I obeyed, waving, hearing their voices change as another ran towards the line.

Later Bracus sent for me.

He stood before his office, a dim place filled with scrolls and tablets containing the accounts and various contracts in which he was interested; details of arrangements with travelling lanistae, records of slaves, agreements with free gladiators. Labeo, the chief doctore of the school, was with him. The instructor watched as, obeying Bracus, I stripped and turned, flexing my muscles, bending, jumping as high as I could into the air.

'Well, Labeo, sword or net?'

The instructor took his time deciding. He felt my shoulders, fingers digging into the flesh, his hands moving to my forearms, my thighs.

'He's big and will get bigger. Those bones are built to

carry weight.' To me he rapped, 'Have you ever fished when a boy? Used a net?'

'No.'

'He could be taught,' said Bracus. 'He's fast at least.'

'There's more to using a net than practice. It takes a special knack and I don't think he's got it.' Labeo stared at me, musing. 'A little too heavy for a Thracian and, anyway, we've plenty of those. He'd be wasted as a pugile, that face has to be saved to win support from the women. A myrmillo, Bracus, or a secutor.'

'A secutor.'

So it was decided.

CHAPTER 9

If I'd worked hard before I worked twice as hard now, different labour but even more demanding. For hours a day I struck at wooden posts wrapped with straw, using a sword twice as heavy as those used in the arena, blunt and with a rounded point. My trainer was a Gaul, old, irascible, his voice as cutting as the whip he used at the slightest provocation.

'Hit it, don't kiss it! I want to see that straw fly!' The cut of his whip emphasised the instruction. 'Harder, Atilus, harder!'

In my imagination the post became a Roman soldier, tall, arrogant.

Flaccus grunted his satisfaction as he moved away to yell at one of the others, to use his whip like a flail.

I paused, wiping sweat from my eyes. Around me in the exercise yard men were busy developing or improving skills. There a retiarius was handling his net as if it were a part of him, the lead-weighted mesh opening to settle, to close and be jerked back by the thong attached to a wrist, the trident held in the other hand to stab, sunlight gleaming from the polished barbs. They, like the sword, were blunted, the weapon extra heavy.

Some distance away a Thracian was weaving, slashing with the curved sica, his small shield an extension of his arm. Next to him a man with a lasso, another with a spear, others hurling small javelins at bales of man-shaped straw; some gaetulians, running to sting like wasps, their darts carrying death. There were dozens of men, filling the yard, the air with their grunts, the smell of their sweat. Men trained to become killers, knowing that, unless they killed, they would die.

Gladiators!

Now I was one of them, a tiro who had yet to have his first fight. Training usually took two years – only a little of that time remained.

'Atilus!' Flaccus came storming towards me. 'Get back to work!'

I suffered the lash of his whip as I had suffered so many other things; the crude horseplay in the hall, the raw, practical jokes. There had been three fights, one of which I had lost, each time spending a period in the stocks where, without food or water, I had roasted in the sun at day, shivered in the chill at night.

Others had not been as fortunate. Rejected, failing, they had vanished, sold to the arena as meat for the beasts. I'd wondered why they hadn't been used as training partners, but, during a period of rest, Flaccus had explained.

'You can't learn anything from an inferior, only a superior. Put good men against bad and they'll become overconfident. They'll lose their edge and, when it comes to the real battle, they'll go down. And there's no profit in wasting time on failures. Either a man makes the grade or he gets sold. Remember that, Atilus, keep it in mind.'

Now he stood over me, his whip busy, his voice a rasping grate in my ears.

'Hit it, man! Think of it as that bitch who got you into this. Hit it!'

The story was known, had been repeated, with sniggers and embellishments, but I'd played along, inventing titivating details.

But remembering Flavia woke desire and I longed for the coming of night when it could be satisfied. Tonight was my turn to be given a woman and I wondered who it would be.

Getia, I hoped – we had something in common. The child swelling her belly, so she had assured me, was mine.

'Change hands.' A flick of the whip opened my ears. 'Use the left and build up that shield-arm. Hit it! Hit!'

I was a willing pupil, the more they could teach me the more I could kill, sending others to bite the sand, each death a step towards the desired rudis, and the freedom it would bring.

To one side a sullen German swore as the whip stung his flesh.

'Do that again and—'

'You'll what?' Flaccus lifted the thong. 'You're soft, man. Soft. Now get in there and work!'

The thong came down with a hiss, the tip curling around the German's head and hitting an eye. Blinded, mad with pain, he turned, his sword raised, sweeping down at the trainer. Had it been sharp it would have sheared the arm from Flaccus's body, but no practice weapon was ever sharp.

I heard the thud, the snap of breaking bone, the trainer's yell.

'Guards!'

They came at the run, lances levelled, arms drawn back for the throw. The German stared at them, saw his death in the winking points and made a mistake. He threw down his sword and stood with folded arms. His injured eye, smeared with blood, oozed a clear liquid.

'Peace!'

His appeal for peace had no effect; no slave could strike a trainer and hope to escape the consequences. He was crucified.

I saw it done, standing with the others, the entire yard filled with watching figures, the guards forming a wall all around. Slaves lashed, not nailed him to the cross, tying his wrists to the cross-beam, setting a block of wood beneath his feet. Suspended he could breathe only by supporting his weight on the block. The constriction of his chest made every breath a struggle and the resultant cramps would turn his muscles into fire.

He would hang, without food or water, until he died.

That night, as Getia was ushered into my room, I could see him by the light of torches. His head had fallen to one side, the features etched with lines of agony, the ruined eye giving him a peculiar, lop-sided appearance. He moaned a little, calling out to his gods in his own tongue, but they were far away across the Rhine and, if they heard, they did not answer.

'Atilus!' Getia came towards me. She was a strong, dark-haired girl, her milk-filled breasts hanging prominently beneath the coarse wool of her gown. 'Atilus, don't look at him!'

I had little chance, the guard closed the door, locking it with a crude jest.

'Ride well, Atilus, you've had plenty of practice at using a sword.'

He was a rough man, but kind in his way, turning a blind eye to minor infractions. Getia had brought a lamp and a flask of wine. She set the lamp on the shelf and put the wine beside the bed. The swell of her belly made her movements awkward.

I had only her word that it contained my child. It could have been anyone's she, like the rest of the females, were passed around as a reward for good behaviour. It was a means both of easing tension and of breeding slaves.

Without ceremony she slipped out of her gown and stood naked before me.

'Atilus?'

It had been a mistake to think of Flavia earlier. Looking at Getia now I remembered the other and felt desire die as I compared the two. One a spoiled bitch, wanton, wilful, yet possessed of charm and seductive attraction, the other a simple girl knowing only how to offer her body, submitting to, rather than enjoying, the embraces offered by various men.

'Atilus, is something wrong?'

'No.'

'You're not looking at me, am I so ugly?' Her hands touched her breasts, her belly. 'Is it because of this?'

'Of course not.' It would have been cruel to be truthful. 'It's just that, well – I'm sorry, Getia.'

'That man then? The one on the cross?' She shook her head. 'Don't think about him. He knew what would happen if he attacked a trainer. Sit down and have some wine.'

It was thin, vinegary, probably supplied by a kitchen slave in return for certain favours, the man risking a whipping in exchange for a moment of lust. The guard too, was probably paid in kind. It didn't matter, slaves survived as best they could.

As I drank I felt her come close to me, felt the heat of her body, the touch of her hand as she ran her fingers through my hair.

'What shall we call it, Atilus?'

'It?'

'The child, silly.' She took my hand and held it against her. Beneath the taut mound I could feel the kick of tiny feet. She was near her time, the prominent nipples on the sagging breasts were moist with oozing liquid. 'It will be a boy and it will grow up to look just like you. Tall, strong, beautiful.' Again she ran her fingers through my hair. 'What shall we call it, my darling?'

'Britannicus.'

'And if it should be a girl?' She gave me no time to answer. 'No, it will be a boy. Sabina, the old woman in the kitchens, promised me that. She gave me a mixture to eat and I've prayed to the gods. It will be a boy, Atilus.'

A boy, a slave, condemned to servitude from the moment

of birth. Never knowing what it was like to run free and wild, the warmth of a family, the comfort of relatives.

My own boyhood had been lonely enough lacking, as I did, brothers and sisters and a close family circle. But I'd had my mother and had known my father and had met the other children of my tribe as an equal. We had played childish games and waged childish wars – what would it have been like had I been a slave?

'Atilus!' Her words came through a fog of time and memory. 'Atilus, please!'

She was swollen, distorted, conscious of her appearance, needing to be reassured that I found her pleasant to my eyes. I dropped my arm around her, cupping one of the full breasts, banishing all thoughts of Flavia as I pressed her to me, kissed her, felt the soft impact of her mouth.

A hungry mouth which triggered an equal demand.

A need.

Rising I stripped and approached as she too rose. She was small, her breasts touched my waist, the curve of her belly low against my thighs. For a moment we clung, awkwardly together then, smiling, she pushed me towards the bed.

'Lie down, darling, you must leave this to me.'

The roof was low, the lamplight dim, against the rafters I could see her hair reflecting little gleams of shifting glow, the tresses framing her face as she leaned over me. Her breasts were succulent fruits which teased my mouth. The heat between her thighs engulfed me, enclosed me in a moist embrace.

'Atilus! My darling!'

She panted as she moved, pressing herself against me, gasping as she flooded my turgid flesh. I reared, clutching her soft femininity, feeling the pulse and eruption of release.

Later, lying with her buttocks pressed against my loins, I heard the German on the cross scream out in his pain.

They let him scream for three days then broke his legs with an iron bar so that, no longer able to support his weight, he quickly died.

Dead, he was left hanging as a grim example, filling the yard with the stench of corruption, his face, tilted, eyes staring, shrinking to the likeness of a skull.

The night of the day they took him down Veianius used me to slake his lust.

He was a big man, a myrmillo, proud and arrogant, a bully who strutted through the hall. The position of gladiators among themselves was well defined; tiros had no prestige, spectati, those with one or more successful fights to their credit, could, and did, order them about. They, in turn, were bossed by the veterani, old hands who were first class fighters. I was a tiro, Veianius a spectati.

He caught me by the arm as I passed the end of the table at which he sat throwing dice.

'Atilus, I need your heathen luck. If I throw Venus I win.'

Three sixes which he didn't make. Cursing he threw aside the cup.

'The gods are against me, or perhaps I misread the omens. Not Venus, but Apollo, eh, lads?'

They laughed, but there was something ugly in the sound and I guessed that they knew more than I suspected. Rough humour always stood poised on the edge of cruelty, jokes based on another's pain and gladiators, of all men, were the least gentle.

'Apollo,' said Veianius again. 'A smooth, tender creature with the cheeks of a woman. Soft and enticing and offering great promise of joy. Things to touch and fondle.'

He wasn't talking about my face.

'Remember how he ran down the line?' One of the others leaned forward over the table, leering. 'He haunted my sleep for a week. Such dreams!'

'And such a bloodied nose, Priedens!' A man, scarred, his

teeth broken snags, laughed as he looked at me. 'You tried to win the prize and lost.'

Veianius said, slyly, 'One battle does not decide a war. Atilus is like a woman who needs to be persuaded. Once the thing is done they are grateful.'

'And eager for more,' yelled the scarred man. 'The first time is always the hardest, but once the seal is broken the treasure lies for all to take.'

'You should know, Hilarius!'

The talk buzzed, but the ugliness remained. Veianius dropped his arm over my hips, his hand pressing, squeezing. I tried to back away and was prevented by others standing close behind. As Veianius rose I spat in his face.

'Roman scum!'

He was free-born, a citizen who had killed a prostitute in a particularly vile manner. Her guild had protested to the magistrates and Veianius had been sentenced to the arena, having to serve two years in the school and three on the sand.

He looked at me, spittle running down his cheeks, then his hand rose, the fingers clenched into a fist, the fist slamming towards my jaw.

I tried to dodge, was stopped by the men gathered behind me, saw a flash of stars as the blow landed. Dazed, half-stunned, I was barely aware of Veianius's shout.

'Into the back, lads. Bend him over and bare that arse. I'm first!'

Held fast, powerless to struggle, I could only submit. I felt the pressure, the penetration, heard the harsh, animal-like rasping of his breath as he used me as he would a woman. When he withdrew the hands holding me slackened a little as others demanded their turn. I twisted, kicked, heard the high-pitched scream of a man as he doubled, clutching at his groin. Another reared back to save his eyes and I lowered my fingers and stabbed at his throat instead.

A harsh voice cut through the babble, the confusion.

'Hold! What goes on here?'

Labeo, attended by guards, attracted by the noise was standing before us. He glanced at me, then at Veianius, knowing what had happened. A common enough episode, but there had been too much noise, and he had little sympathy for Greek love, less for sexual rivalries. Such things lowered the efficiency of the school.

'Atilus, all of you, get to your rooms.' The snap of his whip emphasised the command. 'Move!'

The next day, after breakfast, I made a request of Flaccus. He frowned, nursing his broken arm, then agreed. Labeo repeated the frown.

'Fight? You're not ready yet and won't be until I say so.'

'Please, Domini. I want to be paired against Veianius.'

A willing fighter was worth ten who had to be lashed into combat and the instructor guessed my reasons. Bracus pursed his lips as he heard them.

'It's unusual, Labeo. A small thing like that – it isn't cause enough to match a man out of his class. And another thing, Atilus has been trained as a secutor. Veianius is a myrmillo.'

'It doesn't matter, Domini,' I said. 'I can—'

Labeo cut me short. 'It could be an advantage. Veianius will be expecting the usual responses and it's up to Atilus to see he doesn't get them. And a grudge fight always gets the crowd. I say let him have a go. We have a munera due in two days time. Priedens can be put against a retiarius and Atilus can take his place against Veianius.'

'Well—' Bracus was uncertain. His reputation was at stake and more. Gladiators were expensive items of property and not to be wasted. 'Quintus won't like it.'

'Quintus isn't here,' pointed out the instructor. 'If Atilus wins he'll thank you for pushing him forward, if he goes down then, at least, he'll know the value of his investment.' Smiling he added, 'I like the idea. Veianius is getting too big for his boots lately and needs to be taken down a little. Matching him against a tiro will do just that. We can arrange things so that if either of them go down nothing will be lost.'

A faked cut, a bribed charonian, the supposedly dead man dragged from the arena to be sold to a lanista in another part of the country. It was insurance in case the crowd showed no mercy.

But I didn't think of that. I was twenty years old and, in two days time, I intended to kill a man.

CHAPTER 10

It was the custom for the holder of a munera to give a feast in the amphitheatre on the eve of the games. All contenders were present by right and the public were admitted, most of them bringing presents of food and wine together with cheap trinkets and lucky charms. Degenerates mostly, men and women who slavered over the gladiators, touching them, patting, hands straying to private parts.

I pushed away a painted matron and then a raddled old man, both of whom offered money if I would accommodate them. The man seated opposite me at the long, narrow table shook his head.

'You were too quick to refuse, Atilus. Money's always useful, favours too, it always helps to have friends when you're down and needing mercy.'

'From them?'

'From anyone.' He was cynical. 'And the more influence they have the more they can help. That woman, for example, those clothes she was wearing didn't come cheap. She could have sons, certainly a husband, maybe a lover or two on the side. She'll have relatives and friends and, if you made up to her, she'd get them shouting for you from the tiers.'

I glanced to where she was walking off with a scarred pugile.

'Her?'

'Well, maybe not her, but there'll be others and you have to think of these things.' He helped himself to more wine. 'You're young, Atilus, but you'll learn – given luck.'

Elebus was a velite, fighting with a spear attached to his body by a thong. He was built like a whip, his stringy muscles barely knotting under his skin, his face long and mournful. He was also getting very drunk.

'To youth, Atilus. You have it, I do not, well, that's life.'

'You want to go easy on that stuff.'

'The wine?' He shrugged. 'Eat and drink, my friend for tomorrow – you know how it goes.' He leaned back looking at the gladiators, the others. 'Look at them, mourners at a funeral. That's how it all began, you know, the ritual feast to speed the departed soul. Then fighters were used so as to give the dead man the company of slain warriors. Now we have the ludi, the games. A bigger feast, Atilus, over a bigger grave. The grave of Rome.'

'Careful!' He had spoken too loudly, heads had turned in our direction.

'I worry you?' Elebus grinned. It was a grimace barren of humour. 'You're lucky, Atilus. Young and strong and not cursed as I am with the ability to read the future. You doubt it? Give me your hand.'

He took it, filling the cupped palm with wine, brooding as he stared at the ruby liquid.

'A long life,' he muttered. 'Successful as these things are measured. There is pain and hurt but there is also joy. Beware of men who smile too easily. Of those who talk too much. Stay clear of women who make promises and of boys who want to get too close. Keep edge and point sharp and your mind on your opponent at all times. And always remember to smile at the crowd.'

He burped and released my hand, wine running like thin blood over the palm. An omen I didn't care for, I wiped it clean on my short robe as he filled bowls and passed me one.

Holding it to my lips, only pretending to drink, I looked around.

Lower down the table Thracians and Gauls had eaten well if not wisely. Some Germans who had arrived with a travelling lanista swilled wine with careless disregard for the morrow. A pair of Greek lovers made tender farewells, each touching the other on the face, tears in their eyes. A young fool who had volunteered to fight freed his slaves in anticipation of possible death. Veianius sat, boasting, attended by a cluster of doting women.

'You want to see slaughter? I'll give it to you, young tripe spread out for your inspection. A pretty boy biting the sand and whining as he feels his hurts. Back me with every sestertii you can raise if you want to make some easy money and, when you collect your winnings, remember the man who earned it.'

'We'll remember you, Veianius,' cooed one, a hard-eyed vulture from a decadent family. 'There'll be a gold piece just for you riding on the outcome.'

'You can collect afterwards,' said another suggestively. 'The money and other things.'

'Soft bodies on which to practice,' said a third, younger, her cheeks flushed with wine and passion. 'Targets for your sword. Why not flesh it now, Veianius? Bury it deep as you will tomorrow.'

An invitation he didn't refuse. Elebus sneered as he staggered from the table, one arm over the woman's shoulder, his feet unsteady from wine.

'To hear Veianius talk you'd think he was immortal like the gods. But the arena isn't a bed and his opponent not as eager to take his thrust as those stupid cows.'

'I know.'

'That's right, you're fighting him, I'd forgotten.' Elebus swallowed his wine. 'You're coming on late so remember to keep your back to the sun. He has a trick of twisting his blade so as to catch the light, when he does get ready for an attack.'

'Anything else?' The man was old in terms of the arena and, while low in the gladiatorial hierarchy, would have learned by watching.

'Watch his right foot. When it digs into the sand step to one side. It means that he's going to lunge forward and slam you with his shield. Do you want a woman?'

Startled by the change of subject I shook my head.

'You're wise. Some men think it's good to ease the flesh and to clear their minds. Others consider it best to conserve their strength. Wine and women, my friend, the ruin of many a good gladiator. Remember that if you can.'

'And you?' I frowned as he rose, swaying, waving at a bedizened slut who came running to his side, wetness on her lips, thin cheeks ravaged by dissipation. 'Why don't you take your own advice?'

'Atilus – do you think I read your future and not my own?'

A remark I remembered the next day when I saw his body dragged from the arena, intestines like bloody ribbons as they trailed over the sand.

'Veianius, Atilus, get ready. You're on next.' Labeo stood by the portal of the Gate of Life staring at the slaves busy cleaning the arena. Around us hummed the apparent confusion of controlled activity, trainers, slaves, those who worked in the amphitheatre milling like ants. The air stank of the stench of blood and beasts, of sweat, smoke and body oil. Close to us the Master of Games clapped his hands and nodded. 'Out! Move!'

I ran out onto the sand.

The arena!

Trapped in the oval bowl the air was hot, stale, foetid. The sun, just past the zenith, blazed with a savage heat which the awnings did little to dispel and here, on the floor of the amphitheatre, there was no protection at all.

The arena at Cuneo, like that at Vienne, was small, built of wood, the tiers rising steeply, packed now with avid faces.

On the podium the editor of the games slumped in his chair like a bloated toad. I'd studied him during the ceremonial march, a hard man and a stranger to mercy. He'd paid for the display and wanted his money's worth. Ambitious and mean he'd dedicated the games to the Emperor at the same time using them to gain popular support for his ambitions to high office.

He had stinted on the expense, the initial acrobats had been poor, the trinqui few, the bestiarii not of the best. Need, not desire, had forced him to provide a minimum of skilled gladiators.

'Veianius!' The shrill voice of a woman called from the upper tier. 'We're with you, Veianius!'

Other voices followed, a roar of support from those who had backed the known contender. None called my name, I was unknown, a tiro who, they thought, had been led to the slaughter. A certain victim who would shortly bite the sand.

My equipment aided that belief.

The differences between the armour of a secutor and a myrmillo were small but to the knowledgeable highly important. Veianius's shield was larger, heavier, his helmet a different pattern to my own and a band of metal was fastened around his lower torso; protection which rose from his belt to half-way up his chest. Our swords, sandals, the single greave we each wore on our left shin, were the same as was the armour on our right arms, a series of overlapping metal plates which ran from shoulder to wrist. I had no body-armour and my helmet had a wide brim which sloped back over my neck, the lattice which normally covered the face had been removed for this special occasion. An asset despite the danger to my eyes; the removal had given me better vision.

The largest difference between the two types of gladiators lay in the men themselves. Myrmillones, sometimes called Gauls, were 'heavies', strong, bulky men with massive arms and shoulders, thick-set bodies and columnar thighs. Secutors were 'chasers' needing to be quick, lithe and agile. But my one advantage was more than counter-balanced by my lack of experience.

Labeo had accompanied me, standing behind with a slave attending a brazier into which had been thrust long irons fitted with wooden handles. The metal was made red hot and would be thrust against my bare flesh if I flagged in my willingness to fight.

Flaccus stood behind Veianius, also with a brazier, also with a slave. The slaves would use the irons, the trainers standing well back and giving their instructions.

'Right, Atilus,' snapped Labeo. 'In!'

I edged forward, conscious of the watching crowd, men and women leaning forward, mouths open, eyes feral as they waited for the sight of blood. The shield, held close, covered my left side from just below the shoulder to inches above the knee. The sword rested close to it, the point held a little upwards, ready to thrust or cut as the situation demanded.

Facing me Veianius grinned in his conviction that I was easy prey.

'Your face, Atilus, I'll change it for you. Take out an eye or lop off that nose. They won't call you pretty after today.'

He talked to frighten, to slow my reactions, to distract. I saw his right foot shift a little, moving forward to dig into the sand and remembered what Elebus had said. Advice from a dead man and not to be ignored.

As Veianius lunged forward, to slam his shield against mine, to knock me down with his superior weight, I sprang to one side, the sword lifting, falling, the point slicing a line over the back of his shoulder. It left a shallow wound which didn't affect the efficiency of his shield arm, but which drew blood.

'Habet!'

Veianius didn't need the roar of the crowd to tell him he

was wounded. He poised, snarling, inching forward as I backed. Behind me came the rattle of metal and Labeo's warning.

'Atilus, in!'

Unless I obeyed I would be burned, but to obey was to risk too much. Circling I moved from the brazier, caught the shift of Veianius's eyes, and turned, sword swinging, hearing the ring of metal as I dashed the iron from the slave's hand.

A move which almost cost me my life.

Veianius was big, heavy, but he could move fast when he had to. He came rushing, sword lifted, falling, the edge biting into the upflung edge of my shield. A hail of blows which numbed my arm and sent me staggering back, to tread on a patch of hidden blood, to slip and fall to one knee.

'Habet! Hoc habet!'

The roar came again like the surge of waves on a shore, the crowd rising, yelling as Veianius came at me, hammering, beating down my shield.

I was wounded, blood running from my shoulder, but though down I wasn't out no matter what the crowd may have thought. Hunched under the shield I concentrated on defence, using my sword only to knock aside the blade which stabbed at my eyes, bringing down the edge on the inch of flesh which showed above his greave.

Another minor cut, but it gave me time to regain my feet, to retreat, to stand panting, blood running from my gashed shoulder to puddle on the sand.

Veianius came on again.

He was more than confident now, certain of victory, convinced that he could afford to toy with me, to drag out the combat. His voice was a sneer as he beat at me with his sword.

'You should have stuck to the kitchens, Atilus. You'll never make a fighter. You're beaten. You're going down. Soon you'll be begging for mercy but you won't get it. Where do you want it? In the guts? In the chest? Shall I take off a hand?' His grin was vicious. 'Maybe I'll geld you.'

I said nothing, continuing to back, moving in a circle, using my sword not to attack but to break the force of his blows. Delaying tactics which the crowd recognised and didn't like.

I heard their jeers, a shrill voice calling from the tiers.

'Stick it into him, Veianius, and tonight you can stick something else in me!' A woman's voice followed by the deeper bellow of a man.

'Rip out his guts! Let's see the colour of his tripe!' A patrician who would have a slave whipped if the man nicked him while shaving his fat cheeks, but who thought nothing of another's pain.

I ignored him as I ignored Labeo's voice, the slave standing ready with the hot irons.

And then, all it once, it came.

There is a state of mind essential to anyone who fights in the arena. A concentration, a dedication, a wild determination to win, to kill. Anger and hate could help bring that about, but rage had to be controlled, channelled, mastered and used as a tool. A tool which I had been slow to master.

But it came. It came.

The roar of the crowd dimmed, the faces, the straining bodies, all vanished from my sight. Now there was nothing but Veianius, a man who had used me as the legionaries had used my mother.

A Roman!

And, for almost two years now, I had been trained to kill.

My body took over, divorced of the hampering need of thought, intention translated immediately into action. My shield lifted, slammed aside his sword my own blade poised, levelled, darting towards his right eye as I lunged forward.

Veianius was fast, the point took him on the cheek as his

head reared back, sharp steel opening the flesh and turning his cheek into a crimson mess.

My shield held back his right arm, the hand holding the sword, but lifting it had left me open. I felt the bruising impact of his shield as he slammed it against me and then I was dancing backwards, each breath an ache, the taste of blood in my mouth.

'You bastard! You'll pay for that!'

Rage, but a different kind to my own, a fury which engulfed him but robbed him of calculated thought. Like a storm he attacked me, his blade a wheel of light, the edge turning, blunting as he hammered at my shield.

Again I broke free, gaining space between us, my own sword catching the sunlight and reflecting it back into his eyes. An old trick and one he should have known how to avoid, but anger and previous certainty had made him careless.

As he blinked I moved in.

The armour on our right arms covered and protected only the outside of the limb. Inside, where straps held the covering fast, was open flesh. Higher up the armpit was a vulnerable target. The armpit and the face; covered as he was by the shield it was the only other vulnerable point. But his rear was naked from nape to kidneys, from waist to ankle.

I glided in, moving poised on the balls of my feet, sacrificing the power of my blows for the sake of greater mobility. Again I thrust at his eyes, turning the thrust to a sidewise cut at his arm as his shield lifted, feeling the grate of metal as the edge caught the overlapping plates. A move which turned me so as to present my right side to the hammer-blow of his shield.

A blow I had anticipated, one which hurt only air as I sprang back, then forward again to cut at his back, blood welling from a deep gash in the bunched muscles of his previously injured shoulder.

A wasted blow, I had hoped to chop his spine but he had given me no time to aim. Already he was spinning, the shield out-thrust, beating against my own, the force of the blow sending me staggering to one side.

To tread on buried excreta.

To slip and fall.

I looked at death standing over me.

The jar of the fall had caused the sword to slip from my sweaty palm, before I could regain it Veianius was on me, his sandal clamping my wrist, his sword raised as, grinning, he stared down at me.

'Too bad, Atilus!'

With his foot on my wrist I couldn't signal with my right hand for mercy. My left still held the shield. I could throw it aside and lift my hand, but to do so was to invite death.

Death or worse.

An agreement had been made and Veianius might follow it, but the fake cut he would give me, while not killing, could cripple. A slash across the eyes would leave me blind. A chop at the tendons, would leave me crippled, maimed, doomed to be put among the trinqui. And he would do just that.

But I still had the shield.

As Veianius turned towards the editor, smiling, lifting his sword, I slammed the edge between his thighs.

He was stocky, I had long arms. He stood with legs straddled – the blunted edge of metal caught his testicles with crushing force.

As he doubled I rolled, tearing free my wrist, snatching up the sword and knocking him down so that he, not I, lay on the sand.

The crowd went wild!

They rose, yelling, filling the amphitheatre with cheers, with the roar of my name.

'Atilus! Atilus! Atilus!'

From the fickle crowd whose loyalty was governed by

their bets, by the mood of a moment, came adulation.

I had amused them.

I was their hero.

And, losing, Veianius had cost them money. On all sides came the downward stab of thumbs demanding his death.

'Atilus!' He stared up at me, face contorted, sweat mixed with the blood giving him the appearance of a painted clown. 'The deal! Remember!'

I was kinder than he would have been. As the editor added his decision to that of the crowd I swung the sword and opened Veianius's throat from ear to ear.

CHAPTER 11

Bracus Murallius was annoyed and showed it. Back at the school, he said, curtly, 'There was an arrangement made, Atilus. Why didn't you keep it?'

'Domini, I made a mistake.'

'An expensive one. Veianius was a good gladiator.'

'But not good enough,' rumbled Labeo. 'He lost.'

'By a fluke. There was no need to have killed him. Atilus, you went against my instructions. You know the penalty for that.'

The stocks, the scourge, even, perhaps, the cross. In imagination I heard again the screams of the German, remembered the way he had died.

'Domini, it was a mistake,' I insisted, lying. 'I misjudged and cut too deep.'

'He was carried away,' said Labeo, defending me. 'I saw his face. But he's a good fighter – not once did I have to use the irons. He'll learn, Bracus. He'll learn.'

'Perhaps, but not here.' The lanista was firm. 'I'm selling him to an agent from Rome.'

'Quintus?'

'Is dead, killed by a lion which broke from its cage. Under the terms of our contract I take over. Marcus Cadius was impressed by Atilus and has offered a good price. I've accepted it.' Bracus looked at me. 'You're lucky, Atilus. Now go and get those wounds seen to.'

I'd been hit three times, once on the shoulder and a couple of minor cuts I hadn't noticed at the time. My chest hurt a little and I suspected a cracked rib. A suspicion verified by the medicus attached to the school.

Hasrah was a Jew, lacking the reputation of Greek physicians, but a good enough doctor in his way. He grunted as I flinched beneath his probing fingers.

'Not broken but cracked, I'd say. I'll bind them tight and you'll have to take things easy for a while. Now let me see that shoulder.'

The wound was deep, blood welling from the gash despite the bandage wrapped over it. Hasrah threw the soggy mess away, called for water and washed his hands in the bowl held by a slave. Hasrah, himself, was free, a Roman citizen born in Antioch who had studied in Egypt and Greece, staying a while in Spain before moving to Italy.

He sucked in his breath as he examined the wound.

'Bad?'

'It could have been worse, Atilus. The muscle is bruised and cut, but no serious damage has been caused. You'll be stiff for a while, but it will pass.' He probed, then made his decision. 'I'll have to cauterise in order to seal the flesh. Alus, prepare the wine.'

The wine – the searing irons already stood in a brazier. I looked at the goblet of wine which the slave handed to me.

'Opium,' he explained. 'Hasrah believes in it. It'll put you to sleep and help with the pain.'

This sounded like weakness, it was the pride of gladiators that they could take wounds without complaint, but Hasrah was more practical.

'Sleep is the best healer, Atilus, but a man in pain finds it hard to rest. He twitches, moves, breaks open his wounds. The opium will dull your senses and give you pleasant dreams. Alus, the iron!'

Lying face down on the couch I gritted my teeth as Hasrah held it close. I could feel the heat of it on my back, the pressure of his fingers as he held tight the lips of the cut.

The iron touched!

I jerked, sweating, the nails digging into my palms as I clenched my fists, smelling the stench as the hot metal traced its way over the lips of the cut, searing, fusing them together. Blood thundered in my temples and blackness edged my vision then, suddenly, it was over and I lay gasping like a newly landed fish.

The opium brought, not pleasant dreams, but a nightmare.

I was back in the arena, Veianius facing me, his sword cutting, laughing as he shredded my body. Back in Britain looking at the body of my mother. Back in the villa of my late master, looking at his wife, a woman who sprouted snakes in place of her curls and came at me with curved hands tipped with reeking claws.

A one-eyed German shrieked as he writhed on a cross.

Blood ran from the lacerated back of a soldier.

Intestines trailed on the sand.

Cobwebs embraced me, held me fast as vicious barbs neared my eyes, the trident backed by a grinning face. I heard the roar of the crowd, the sound of my name.

'Atilus!'

I stirred, turned and felt the pull at my shoulder, agony washing over me like liquid fire. In the yellow gleam of lamplight Hasrah's face loomed close.

'Atilus?'

'What is it?' My mouth was parched, I gulped at the water he handed to me in a bowl. 'What do you want?'

'Can you stand? Move?'

Nausea gripped me as I rolled from the couch, sending me double, clinging to the edge of the couch for support. My ears rang and my vision was blurred, after-effects of the opium, I guessed. A bucket stood to one side and I ducked my head, the water helping to clear my brain.

Straightening I looked around.

The infirmary of the school was small, dark, the roof low. Around me lay limp figures, most silent, others, the weaklings, moaning from the pain of their wounds. They had reason to moan. One man had lost an arm, the stump seared and blackened with hot irons. Another had lost the entire side of his face, the flesh cut away to reveal his teeth and jaw. A third had received a blow on the mouth which had severed his lips and smashed his teeth. The rest would have sword cuts, severed tendons, broken bones. Only those who had a chance to survive were catered for, the hammer took care of the rest.

'Atilus?'

I shook my head, breathing deeply, my senses still fuzzy. The air didn't help. It was dank, heavy with the stench of blood and sweat, vomit and urine, excreta and the odour of charred meat. A glowing brazier stood against a wall and, looking at it, I shuddered.

'Atilus, it's Getia. She's been asking for you.'

'Me?'

'You.' Hasrah was patient. 'I think you should see her.'

He led me from the infirmary to where the woman's quarters lay beside the kitchens. It was still dark though nearing dawn, a pale wash of light dimming the stars. A guard grunted as we approached.

'Hasrah?'

'Yes. I'm needed.'

The man grunted again, but let us pass. In a small, overcrowded room Getia lay naked on a cot.

'Atilus!' She smiled, raising her hands towards me. 'I knew you would come.'

Her face was lined, haggard, drenched with sweat, perspiration which reappeared no matter how often the old crone wiped it away. She, Sabina, who some rumoured to be a witch, was helpless now in the face of tragedy.

Helpless, but unwilling to admit it.

'The child is overdue,' she whined. 'It should have been born by now. Yet I have a potion which will make all well. A potion and a charm to ease the pain.'

'Out!' snapped Hasrah. 'All of you, out!'

They grumbled, not liking it, reluctant to let a man and a Jew at that abrogate their traditional role. Childbirth lay in the province of women, they should act as midwives, they should bring the new life into the world. What right had any man to rob them of that ancient duty?

'Out!' he snapped again. 'Must I order the guards to use their whips?'

Getia tensed as they left, rearing, her hands gripping mine with bone-bruising strength. Agony made her face ugly, the eyes staring, the mouth open, whimpers torn from her straining throat.

'Scream,' ordered Hasrah. 'Shriek if you want to, you're no gladiator with pride to uphold. Scream, my dear, it may help.'

'No!' Her head rolled from side to side on the sweat-drenched pillow. 'I carry a gladiator's son, I must not weaken him.'

But she was weak herself. Too weak. The labour had lasted too long and Hasrah shook his head as he examined her.

'When the next pain comes, my dear, bear down. You understand?' He touched the bunched muscles of her thighs. 'And try to relax. Tensing your muscles narrows the opening. Help her, Atilus!'

I tried, gripping her hands, smoothing her hair, touching her cheeks, wishing that there was more I could do.

Understanding, for the first time, the travail of a woman in labour.

I'd suffered pain, the cut of a sword, the sear of hot irons, but they had been transistory things, felt and then over, the nagging ache only something which would vanish in time. Her agony had lasted for hours, days, a kind of pain I couldn't begin to understand but, looking at her, could appreciate.

'Atilus! Do you love me? Tell me you love me!'

Hasrah was watching, listening, his eyes softening as I answered.

'Yes, darling, of course I love you. Getia, my sweet, please!'

Please bear the child, my seed grown into largeness in the dark interior of your womb, my child to run and walk in the sun. And live, Getia! Live!

Love comes unexpectedly, flowering in unusual places. I had taken her, used her, enjoyed the relaxation offered by her body, but now, looking at her, feeling the clutch of her hands, something changed. The object of lust became a person, an individual, a woman to be cherished, to be held in tender regard.

As she strained I strained with her. As she sagged, limp, gasping with pain, I felt the agony also, sharp in imagination, the worse because I could do nothing to ease her anguish.

'Hasrah!' I spoke to him quietly in a corner of the room. 'Is there nothing you can do? The opium?'

'It wouldn't help.'

'But you could try!'

'Do you think I wouldn't have used it before now if it was of use?' His voice was sharp, softening as he explained. 'The trouble is that the opening is too small. The head can't pass through.'

'But she'll die!'

'Perhaps.'

'And the child?'

He said, flatly, 'There is something I could do. I could open her belly as was done to the mother of Julius Caesar. She will die, of course, but the child might live.'

A baby without a mother – what would become of it?

'Is there nothing else?'

Hesitating he said, slowly, 'Only one other thing. I could destroy the child, dismember it and draw the pieces through the opening. I saw it done in Egypt, a similar case, the pelvis of the mother too small to allow the passage of the infant. It's the only alternative, Atilus, and it is for you to decide. The mother or the child, the choice is yours.'

A choice I hesitated to make, but there could be no delay, Getia was getting weaker each moment.

'Save the mother, Hasrah. Save her!'

She gripped my hands again when I returned to her side as Hasrah went to collect his instruments. Through the cracks in the door I could see the glowing light of the strengthening day. From the kitchens came small sounds, the rattle of pots, the voices of slaves, the grate of shovels as they cleared the fires. Little things which seemed to be far distant, to belong to another world.

'Atilus, the child?'

'Everything will be all right, Getia. Hasrah will see to it.'

'And later?' Her fingers tensed, closed, became like steel rods as she strained. 'Atilus!'

'Scream, Getia. Scream!'

Blood ran from her bitten lips and her grip purpled my nails, but she didn't scream. She, like the gladiators, had her pride.

As she relaxed I spoke to her, soothing words which painted an impossible dream. I would fight and win and keep on winning until I was given the rudis. Then I would buy her and free her and take her to Britain where, among my people, she would be safe from the tyranny of Rome.

'Us, Atilus, together?'

'For always.'

'And you will love me?'

'For always.'

'For as long as I live.' She smiled and, suddenly, was beautiful. 'I can't ask for more than that, darling. I can't—'

Then again there was the pain, the whimpering, the agony of what tore at her from within.

An agony Hasrah worked to destroy.

I didn't look at him as he worked, nor at the tools he used, the slender rods with sharp curves, the hooks, the crescent-shaped blades. Blood ran over the cot, staining the bare wood between her thighs, flesh and bone dragged from her belly to be thrown aside. But, at last, it was over.

Panting, outraged flesh demanding the release of sleep, she looked at me with sunken eyes.

'Atilus, the child?'

'Dead.' She had to know, but she had already guessed.

'A boy?'

'A girl.' The lie was unimportant, but it could help.

'A girl.' Her sigh held regret and yet also a note of relief. 'Perhaps it is for the best. A slave – that is no life for any woman. Atilus . . .'

She slept, dulled by opium, and freeing her grip I rose to stare bleakly about the room.

It was small, square not oval, yet it was as much an arena as any amphitheatre ever built. The battle of life and death had been waged in it, the struggle to survive, lost. On the sand the enemy was visible, victory a matter of skill and endurance. Here the enemy had been small, contained, loved even as it had tried to kill.

Had killed.

Getia died within the week, her lips cracked, eyes glazed, skin burning with fever.

Ten days later I was in Rome.

CHAPTER 12

Rome!

The heart of the empire, where ruled the master of the world. It sprawled on seven hills, temples and palaces built of marble flaunting on the heights, the valleys crammed with houses, tenements, slums, all cut with narrow, winding streets on which no wheeled traffic was permitted during the day. We reached it from Ostia, the city's sea-port, having travelled down the west coast of Italy in a vessel loaded with hides and beans. Marcus Cadius took me immediately to the place which was to be my home.

The Great School, situated near the via Labican, was one of four Imperial gladiatorial schools in the environs of the city, the others being the Gallic, the Dracian, and an establishment restricted to the training of bestiarii. If the school at Cuneo had been a workshop then the Ludus Magnus was a factory; its product a stream of men trained for the arena.

I had arrived at a good time. The great naumachia recently held by Claudius had drained the prisons of criminals and the schools of gladiators so that fighters were in short supply.

Icelus told me about it.

He was from Crete, tough, sturdy, a myrmillo. A wound caked his right thigh with crusted scabs and he had lost the lower part of his right ear, an old wound which he fingered as he talked. My shoulder, though healing well, was still stiff and the instructor had decided that I should wait before being put to work.

'It won't be long, Atilus, but Primus is fair, he likes to give a man a chance. Anyway, it's no sport for the crowd if a combat is too one-sided.' Icelus stretched his legs before him. 'Make the most of it while you can.'

We sat on a bench, backs to a wall warmed by the afternoon sun, resting after a spell at exercise. Before us in the yard men struck at posts, sprang over weighted thongs lashed at their ankles, ducked beneath swinging weights. One was slow and Icelus chuckled as he was dragged from the area to be dumped, unconscious and bleeding, to one side.

'He'd better not be as slow in the arena. A blow like that could have taken off his head.'

'Tell me about the naumachia. Were you there?'

'Me and everyone else they could get.' Icelus stretched again. 'It was held on the Fucine Lake. Claudius had had a channel dug to drain it and celebrated its completion with a big naval battle. He had two fleets each of twenty-five vessels, one called the Rhodians the other Sicilians. He got almost two thousand prisoners to fight in them under the command of gladiators, and each vessel was filled with slaves at the oars. I guess that half a million people must have watched from the surrounding hills and a stack of babies were born in the hospital he set up. If, in later years, Atilus, you meet men named Fucinus or girls named Fucina, you'll know their age. The Emperor insisted that they all be called that.'

'The fight?' Icelus was rambling.

'I'm coming to it.' He tugged at his shorn ear. 'There was a little trouble to start with. We'd given the usual salute and Claudius made a joke of it so the boys reckoned that he'd pardoned them and refused to fight. That made Claudius mad and he hopped down from his throne and started shouting and threatening as if he'd gone crazy. He wasn't joking, either, he'd had detachments of guards with ballistae set around the lake and he could have burned us all. Anyway, after a while, we agreed to fight and on the signal we went at it. You ever been in a sea-fight, Atilus?'

'No.'

'Stay away from them if you can. They're murder. On the sand you've got a chance to move and duck and you know who your opponent is. On the deck of a ship it's just a madhouse. First you try to ram your opponent and, if you do, then you run over the planks dropped from your bow to the other ship's side. If you can't manage to ram then you bank oars, smash those of the other ship, lower your own and run over them. Either way it's bad. Men waiting, yelling, swords everywhere, noise, blood—' He broke off, shaking his head. 'A real mess. Nothing scientific about it. You can't use any real skill and tricks are a waste of time. It's just a matter of cut and thrust and hope that no one gets you before you get them.'

'Like a war?'

'I guess so, but if that's war then I can do without it. Any fool can swing a sword, but it takes training to know how to do it properly. A man gets to know what to expect, but those criminals were amateurs and as unpredictable as tiros. They had nothing to lose, Claudius had promised that those on the winning side would be given their freedom, and they fought like wildcats. That's how I got this wound. One of them had gone down and he played dirty. He cut me before I could see him.'

Icelus sounded aggrieved, a professional falling victim to an amateur, his sense of propriety outraged by what he considered to be an insult to his pride.

'I got him in turn, though,' he added. 'Took off the bastard's hand with a single stroke.'

He told me more, of the five thousand injured men later treated, the discovery that the channel had been dug too shallow and needed more work.

And of a rumour he'd picked up from an instructor.

'We're going to have more trouble with Claudius,' he

prophesied, grimly. 'The man's crazy and doesn't know when to stop. I did hear they're making up a stack of old Etruscan weapons and armour to fit out a bunch of men for a general skirmish. A fine prospect – we might as well have joined the legions!'

The rumour turned out to be true. Claudius had constructed a wide pontoon bridge across the end of the lake and had arranged for two forces of men to fight on it. One was dressed and equipped as Etruscans, using double-bladed axes, lances and leaf-shaped swords of bronze. The others came out as Samnians. I was one of them.

The armour was heavy. I held a cuirass, a big shield embossed with legendary figures, a helmet adorned with a sheaf of plumes, greaves, a sword longer than I was used to. In effect we were staging a reconstruction of an ancient war from Rome's early history when Horatius had held a bridge against invading forces.

A titivation for the Emperor.

He sat on a throne covered with cloth of gold, a chaplet of laurel on his balding head, the toga doing nothing to disguise the lumpy shape of his body. A weak-looking, almost insignificant man who touched his lips often and craned his head, blinking in the sunlight. It was hard to remember that he had conquered Britain and had later received Caractacus when he was brought as a captive to Rome.

The woman at his side was a startling contrast.

Agrippinilla was much younger. Her features were regular, coldly beautiful, the figure beneath her stola lushly rounded. She, not Claudius, dominated the double-throne. She, not he, carried the haughty air of a patrician. And, if rumour was to be believed, it was the Emperor's wife who held the reins of power.

At my side Icelus said, 'Don't forget, Atilus, we work together.'

He limped, his wound barely healed, and he was in more than a little pain. Yet his suggested arrangement made good sense. We would each watch out for the other, working as a team instead of as individuals. It might not prove possible, but it was worth a try.

At the signal we began to march, each group moving towards the centre of the bridge which had been widened into an area about three hundred feet wide. Music accompanied us, martial airs played by musicians on the shore, and cheering rose from the watching spectators who covered the nearby slopes.

'Stay away from the edge,' muttered Icelus. 'Once in the water you've got to get back on the bridge. Try to land and the guards will spear you.'

Orders which gave a simple choice; fight, win, stand – or die.

The head of our column reached the widened space and fanned out so as to allow others to get into line. A manoeuvre copied by the Etruscans as they too reached the battle ground. Had either side been a cohort of legionaries they could have won easily, as it was within minutes we were a raging mob.

An Etruscan came running towards me, spear levelled, the head falling as I slashed through the shaft. Another chopped at me with an axe, the blade thudding against my shield, biting deep, the shock of the blow sending stabs of pain from my barely healed wound.

He screamed as my sword rose in an upward swing, blood gushing from his deeply cut arm, the blade descending to hit and drag at the naked flesh exposed at the side of his neck above the cuirass. Before me a Samnian yelled as he hammered at one of the enemy, not seeing the figure crouched low, the leaf-shaped sword lifting to cut at the backs of his knees. I kicked out, felt bone crunch beneath my foot, saw the crouching figure rear and turn with blood streaming from his broken nose.

Icelus killed him with a deft thrust.

'Atilus!'

I spun at the warning, caught the downward cut of a sword on my own, felt the jar and heard the rasp of metal, the clang as the hard-driven blade reached my helmet. A push on my shield and the man was staggering back, thrown off balance, head tilted to expose the throat. My point hit just below the chin, driving deep, a crimson flood spurting as I twisted the blade and jerked it free.

From all sides came the harsh panting of straining men, the clash of swords, the thud of axes, the cries and groans of the hurt and dying.

A savage battle in which each man was alone.

We had sides, but that was all. The training which made the legions the masters of the world was lacking. We had no officers, no discipline, no defensive formation. It was kill or be killed, strike to move and strike again, without plan, without reason other than to survive. Like maddened animals we tore each other apart.

The widened area was now a shambles, the wood stained with puddles of blood, littered with dead and dying. Men fought in pairs, mostly, or in little knots which dissolved to reform, to dissolve again each time smaller than before.

Icelus was down, an Etruscan standing over him, axe raised, the blade poised to split his helmet and the skull beneath. Catching the blow on my shield I thrust at the snarling face, felt splintered teeth grate on the blade, pushed it through to the spine. Falling the man tore the trapped blade from my hand. His discarded axe replaced it the head shearing through a sword arm, cutting into a helmet, a shoulder, the upper rim of a shield as I stood over Icelus swinging the heavy weapon as if it were a twig.

Maniacal strength which drained me, left me gasping as enemies fell away and the Cretian scrambled to his feet.

'Atilus!' I saw the peaked face, the shorn ear. His helmet had been knocked from his skull. 'Slow down, man, are you fighting ghosts?'

Memories of the past, a slope running to a river, warriors fighting and dying beneath the might of Rome.

'You went wild,' he said. 'Just like the Germans do sometimes. They run into battle without armour, crazy, not even feeling wounds. Killing until they are chopped down.' He recovered my sword. It was bent and he stamped on the blade to straighten it. 'Here, use this.'

Throwing the axe at an Etruscan I wiped my palm and gripped the hilt. As Icelus recovered his helmet I looked around. We had almost gained the area, a good push and it would be ours.

'Together, lads!' I shouted. 'Together, now, attack!'

I might as well have shouted to the wind.

Men accustomed to fight alone could not or would not take orders. A few glanced at me, but none assembled in the formation which would give us victory. And, as I watched, the Etruscans came like a flood to cut us down.

'Back to back!' yelled Icelus. 'And may the gods help us now!'

Again came the clash and roar of conflict, gaudy plumes sheared from helmets, sent to fall, to be trodden in the dirt and blood. Men followed, armour ringing, shields like gongs beneath the blows of sword and axe. The broad-bladed spears of the Etruscans were everywhere, digging, cutting, stabbing at faces and eyes, driving into throats, smashing against cuirasses. Only my height saved me, the length of my arm, the trained agility which allowed me to weave and dodge, to hold off the relentless push back towards the water.

But the edge of the platform was a ridge beneath my foot

and I heard Icelus cry out as he fell into the lake. A step and I would follow him. Grimly I fought to maintain my position, metal ringing as I parried a cut, thrust back in turn, felt the shock of impact, heard the grunt of the injured man. A shadow warned me and I turned to avoid the swing of an axe. But I had no chance to dodge the spear which slammed against my shield, and, for a moment I hung as if suspended in the air, then water foamed before my eyes.

The shield held me down. I shed it together with my helmet. I had already lost the sword. I could swim, an ability which saved my life. Others, less fortunate, threshed wildly at the water as they moved back to the platform, clinging to the wood, heads thrown back, mouths open as they gasped for breath.

Easy targets for the Etruscan spears.

Icelus was among them. I saw the sharp point slam into his open mouth, the stained tip which appeared at the nape of his neck. Dead he sank like a stone. Others followed, one man holding up the stumps of his arms from which the hands had been chopped, the water turned crimson as he vanished beneath the surface.

A thrown spear lanced towards me, missed by a fraction as I turned and swam back towards the pontoon over which we had marched.

Reaching it I dragged myself from the water and stood, panting, glancing at the double throne. Agrippinilla saw me and frowned, lifting her hand as if to signal a guard, lowering it as I headed towards the battle. A shield had to be found, a sword or axe, a helmet too and then I could fight on for the freedom Claudius had promised to those who won.

A hope dashed before I had covered a dozen yards.

I heard the shouts, the sudden pound of feet and saw the rush of men coming towards me. Samnians who fled the central area and who carried me with them in their headlong rush.

The Etruscans had won. Claudius granted them all their freedom. A few of the Samnians too – but I wasn't among them.

CHAPTER 13

Against the blue of the sky the lasso was a thin, writhing snake, the loop a falling mouth which threatened to engulf me. Watching it I swayed to my left, saw the sudden jerk as the laquearius changed the direction of its fall, swayed to the right, sword upraised.

Ostorius was clever, his move had been as much of a feint as my own. The noose settled over my sword, fell over my wrist, began to tighten as he jerked at the rope.

It would have tightened if I hadn't lunged forward, shield held close, my sword clashing as it beat against the thrusting trident, knocking it aside.

Too late Ostorius recognised his danger. My foot was on the slack of the lasso, holding it hard against the ground, the attached rope making it impossible for him to retreat. Quickly he tried to shorten the trident, his hand slipping along the shaft, but I gave him no time to recover. My shield hit him, my foot catching his ankle as he staggered, sending him down. Stamping on his wrist I trapped the trident and raised my sword.

'Ostorius, you're dead!' Primus stood a few feet distant on the exercise ground shaking his head. 'Too slow and too clumsy, you'd get the death-sign for sure. What do you think, Gallus?'

Gallus Caecina was old and wise in the ways of the arena, a lanista who had merged with the school, sacrificing independence for security. Now he rubbed thoughtfully at his chin.

'Once the rope was trapped he should have circled Atilus on his shield-side. If he had moved fast enough he could have tightened the noose and had him like a fish on the end of a line.'

Ifs and maybes, but in the arena a man only makes one mistake and, usually, it is his last.

'A rope isn't enough of an advantage against a secutor,' said Primus. 'That wide-brimmed helmet hampers the fall of the noose. A net, now, that's different. Do you think Ostorius would stand more chance against a Thracian?'

'I doubt it. One lucky slash of a sica and the rope would fall apart.'

'But he's more open to the trident.'

'True, and the open helmet tells against him as does the small shield. But a Thracian is fast and it takes time to gather the rope and form a noose. I'd say stick to myrmillones or you could try him against a postulati.'

A postulati wore full armour and carried both a sword and a lead mace. Willing to take on all comers with the weapons of their choice such a fighter made a good show.

But, like a myrmillo, he was relatively slow.

'I'll save him for use against some eques,' decided Primus. 'A man on a horse makes a good show when pulled off and, if he can't lasso the man, he can always try for the beast. Right, Ostorius, back to work. You too, Atilus.'

The problem was one of novelty. The crowd demanded variety and their appetite was insatiable. It was easily provided by animals; ostriches, stags, bulls with sharpened horns, lions, bears, tigers, wild dogs, antelopes – a plethora of beasts used to kill, to fight among themselves, to be speared or filled with arrows, to be dispatched by the bestiarii who were both proud and jealous of their profession.

Men were more limited.

The differences between weapons and armour were carefully judged so as to ensure an exciting combat. Pairs were arranged to provide both titivation and meat for wagers.

The experts had also to be considered, patricians, mostly, men and women devoted to the games who had a sharp eye for skill. Agonestes was one high in their esteem.

He was a Greek, tall, slim, his muscles rippling like water beneath an ivory skin. His hair was golden, tightly curled, his face a chiselled mask of perfection. As a boy he had fished the waters of Rhodes, later taking part in a Jewish uprising. Caught he had been sentenced to the arena.

As a retiarius he was low in the gladiatorial hierarchy. The odds were on him winning, but the Romans loved the sword, the gladius which had given us our name. Short, double-edged, pointed, it had cut and thrust its way across the world, turning a village into an empire.

'Atilus!' He smiled and came towards me. 'Trying to learn my secrets?'

'Just watching.'

'Watching and learning too, I hope.' He smiled as he dropped his hand on my shoulder. The fingers were long, slender, remarkably smooth. He was ten years older than myself. 'A man should never cease to learn, Atilus. When he does he might as well go to the place the gods have prepared for him. Until then—' His fingers tightened a little. 'Life is to be used, my friend. Enjoyed.'

I caught the message in his eyes, the invitation, and knew what he implied. Greek love, common among his people, was rife in the school.

'I could teach you,' he continued quietly. 'The tricks I have learned and other things. Tender things, Atilus, which I know you will enjoy.' His hand slipped from my shoulder and traced a path down my arm. 'Why be lonely, Atilus, when there is no need?'

Primus saved me from the necessity of giving an answer.

'You there!' he roared. 'Atilus! Break it up and get to work. Move!'

He kept me hard at it for the rest of the day, using the sword with either hand, dodging blunted poles thrown like spears, loading me down with armour far heavier than normal and making me jump and spring until I was drenched with sweat, the sting of the lash waiting if I flagged.

Relief came with the setting of the sun, but Primus halted me as I followed the others towards the baths.

'You're good, Atilus, but no man is ever good enough not to learn. You want some advice?'

'Please, Domini.'

He smiled at the use of the title, but I meant it. Primus deserved respect. Twice he had won the rudis each time choosing to stay with the school. Now, too old to fight, he taught others the skills which could save their lives.

'I've noticed how you watch Agonestes. He's a good retiarius, one of the best, but don't make the mistake of thinking you can learn from him. Not as you need to learn, at least. Each man has his own manner of fighting. You, he, everyone. Understand?'

'Explain, Domini.'

He sighed. 'Look, when I was in the arena I faced a man who had a special mannerism. Like me he was a myrmillo. He had a habit of shifting his shield a little before he attacked and, when he did, he always struck from right to left. I saw him do it in practice a hundred times. Well, knowing that, I was confident I had him. Just watch for the movement, dodge the swing and in. Only when it came to it he swung from left to right instead. He almost got me and it was my own fault. I'd been over-confident, I knew just what he was going to do – only he didn't do it. Why, Atilus? Tell me why.'

'He knew you were watching and deliberately faked his practice.'

'Not faked, but a man will often change his style or do the

opposite to what is normal. That's what you've got to learn. Keep dodging a net in a certain way and before long you'll find you've run straight into it. So change, Atilus. Keep them guessing. Right?'

'Thank you.'

'Don't thank me, boy, I'm only telling you what you already know. And one other thing. You want the rudis, don't you?'

The rudis and the freedom which went with it. What else was there to hope for?

'Then you'll have to earn it,' he said as I nodded. 'But you're young yet and mustn't be impatient. I could give you thirty years and I came early to the arena. I remember the Emperor Tiberus – a vicious bastard he was, and Caius Caligula was even worse. I've seen him give life to a broken down hack who dropped at the first stroke, yet others who put on a decent show got the death-sign. And you couldn't rely on his word at all.'

He grinned at an amusing memory.

'I remember one time when a fight had been fixed between five retiarii and as many secutors. The secutors were supposed to take a fall and they did confident that they would be saved. Well, Caligula reneged on the deal. One of the secutors was so annoyed that he sprang up, grabbed a trident and killed all the retiarii. A dirty trick everyone called it, but it was the Emperor's fault. He should have kept his word. That's the trouble nowadays, you can't trust anyone. Well, get off now, Atilus, and remember what I told you.' He frowned as I lingered. 'Something else?'

'I'd like to go to the arena tomorrow. Belbrix is there.'

'So?'

'I'd like to see him work.'

'A bestiarius? What can you learn from him?' Primus frowned, then shrugged. 'Well, I guess there's no harm in it.

You can go along and help the contenders. And, Atilus, don't forget my advice. You'll be fighting soon.'

That would make my tenth fight.

Washing I looked down at a stranger now. The face was hard, the cheeks taut, the left scarred. The eyes were deep-set, brooding, the mouth cruel. My face.

It held the stamp of time which shattered as I plunged my head into the bowl. The scar had come from the fight on the bridge, a wound I hadn't noticed until afterwards. Months ago now, the best part of a year in which I'd changed from a boy into a man.

Seven fights for the school. Nine all told – and another coming up. And, after that, more and yet more, an endless series of combats until I was given my freedom or spilled my life onto the sand. The odds were against me, but as I'd been told twice in a single day, no man was too old or too good to learn.

Perhaps Belbrix could teach me.

He stood in the arena, a stocky man bulging with muscle, the scars of old wounds thick on back and thighs. Leather bound his forearms and calves, more snug around his waist and genitals. Metal bands glinted on his biceps and his hair, thick and long, was held by a gemmed fillet.

A rich man, free, the idol of women.

A master of his craft.

Before him a lion crouched low on the sand. A male, its mane was thick, the tufted tail lashing from side to side. It snarled, fangs gleaming white against the red maw of its mouth. The claws, like sickles, made deep grooves in the grit.

Belbrix edged slowly towards it. He was unarmed, bare hands extended a little from the sides of his body, the fingers making small movements, the elbows twitching, like a bird, an ostrich. A trained killer offering himself as prey.

Beside me Heralis sucked in his breath.

'Two to one the lion gets him, Atilus.'

I ignored the offer, concentrating on the man, the beast. The tail twitched a little faster now, the mouth, gaping, emitted a rasping snarl. Now! Surely now!

But Belbrix made no move other than his slight, forward motion, the jerkings of his arms, his fingers.

The lion stared at him, amber eyes reflecting the light, the upper lip twitching, the paws flexing. Now I saw the loins begin to move a little, quivering from side to side as the body lowered and then, without apparent warning, the creature sprang.

Belbrix moved.

At first I thought he had gone down beneath the claws, then saw him standing to one side, moving even as I watched, leaping to straddle the beast, knotted arms reaching under the lower jaw, elbows digging, muscles straining as he twisted, heaved, face contorted, mouth open as he glared at the sky.

A moment in which both lion and man seemed frozen into immobility, a silence which could be felt, a timeless interval suddenly broken by the snap of bone.

The roar of the crowd greeted the bestiarius as he rose from the dead animal and bowed, waving, smiling at the acclaim.

I had seen, but it wasn't enough, I had to know how.

Belbrix was in the baths attached to the arena, a small place where gladiators could wash and rest and receive massage. The unctore glared at me as I pushed him aside, then saw my face and said nothing. Taking his place I began to massage the knotted muscles of the bestiarius's shoulders.

'Ursus?'

'No, Atilus.'

He turned, glaring. 'What—'

'Relax, I can do this.' My hands delved into his flesh. Hard hands, the fingers firm, and I knew what I was doing. Belbrix grunted as, on his back now, he permitted my ministrations.

'If you're after what I think you are, forget it. I'm not a Greek.'

'Neither am I. I just want to talk.' A vase of scented oil stood to one side, I lifted it, poured a stream on my hands, resumed the massage. 'I watched you kill that lion. I wouldn't have believed it possible. You broke its neck, of course.'

He said, abruptly, 'You're a gladiator.'

'Yes.'

'I think I've seen you fight. Atilus? Atilus? Yes, a few months ago now. Well, what do you want?'

'To learn.'

'From me?'

'From a master. An old trainer of mine once told me that a man could only learn from the best. Well, you're it.'

Flattery, a cheap coin but I had little else.

'You've got the face of a Greek,' he said. 'And you've got the smooth tongue of a Greek even if you aren't one. But you're a fool. Do you really expect me to give you my secrets?'

'No.' I'd surprised him, wary as all bestiarii were he had expected me to probe, to ask how he performed the kill. To gain knowledge which I could pass on to another. A suspicion I set at rest. 'I'm not a bestiarius and I don't know anyone who is. I only want to know one thing. How did you know that the lion was going to spring?'

'If you watched you know.'

'I saw what happened, but that's all. If you hadn't moved

when you did you'd be dead now. How did you know when to jump aside?'

'Why?'

'You fight beasts,' I said flatly. 'I fight men. What you tell me could save my life.'

For a moment he stared at me and then, abruptly, laughed.

'By the gods you've got guts asking me a thing like that. Don't you know – well, never mind. Have you any money? Good. I'll tell you over some wine.'

A gift I could barely afford. Money could only be won from the crowd and donated prizes, kept with the permission of my owner which meant, in effect, that imperial prizes went back into the imperial purse. But I had a little, enough to buy a flagon of good vintage which Belbrix swallowed.

'Not bad,' he said, smacking his lips. 'You know, Atilus, I like you. You've got nerve and you're honest, so listen to this. Every animal has its own ways. Lions, now, most people think they're dangerous and they are. But put yourself in the place of one. You've been trapped, carried for miles in a cage, sent across the sea, hauled to the amphitheatre, kept cooped up for days. There's noise and stinks and confusion all around. You're starved, not too much, but enough to make you restless. Then someone shoves fire under your tail and out you go into the arena. What then?'

'Tell me, Belbrix.'

'You're confused, that's what. You want a place to hide only you can't find one. Nothing's familiar and the smell of death is all around.' Belbrix gulped his wine, refilled his bowl and smiled when I placed my hand over my own. 'That's the style. Keep a clear head before a fight and drink yourself silly after one. Well, I've finished for the day. What were we talking about?'

'Lions.'

'Lions.' He nodded. 'Funny creatures, lions, all the cats

are odd, but they're the best to work with. You know they won't touch a dead man? It's a fact. I remember some trinqui once, a bunch of slaves and a couple of women which could have been used for something better. In fact a couple of the boys – well, that's another story. Still it's a pity to waste good meat. Anyway, they had a real idiot among them. A Christian. You ever heard of them?'

'Vaguely.'

'Mad the lot of them. I'm a tolerant man myself and I don't care what god a man worships, but there are limits. Anyway this man refused to burn incense before the household lares and went around telling everyone not to pay taxes and such. Said that we were all going to be taken up to heaven anyway soon, so why bother? Well, he was denounced as a rebel, given the chance to recant, refused and sentenced. Out he went into the arena and after them came the lions. He must have fainted or something. When we went in to kill the beasts there he was, lying without a scratch on him. When he was pulled to his feet he kept asking where he should sit. The fool thought he'd been killed and gone to wherever it is Christians go to.' Belbrix chuckled. 'He went there soon enough. A couple of horses pulled him apart. The point I'm making is that if you lie still a lion won't touch you. If you run around like crazy they get frightened and unpredictable. You've got to soothe them and make them come to you when you're ready. Are you sure you don't want any of this wine?'

'No, you finish it.'

He did just that, smiling. 'You're generous, Atilus, and I like that. Now listen. A beast or a man it's all the same. You've got to watch and know what you're looking at. Take a lion, it crouches, snarls, lashes its tail, but that doesn't mean a thing. You've got to sense when it's ready to spring and that means reading the signs. The way the muscles bunch under the skin, how it breathes, moves its eyes. It takes time and you can collect a few scars learning, but one day you have it. You know.'

And, knowing, survive.

CHAPTER 14

The day I was due to fight broke warm and clear, only wisps of cloud marring the open expanse of the sky and they quickly vanished as the sun climbed towards the zenith. The munera was a three-day event provided as a gift to the city by Claudius himself. I watched him closely during the opening procession. It was the second day and already he looked tired as he lolled in his marble chair, not even straightening as we stood in array and thundered the traditional salute.

'Ave Imperator, morturi te salutant!'

Greetings from men about to die which he acknowledged with a casual lift of the hand.

As before when I had seen him, Agrippinilla was at his side looking truly regal with her hair piled high and studded with gems, more jewels sewn on her stola. At this near distance I could see that her hands were delicately tapered and that the skin of her throat was smooth and firm. For a moment she looked at me, her eyes casual, then glanced to where Narcissus, Claudius's freedman, offered his master a goblet.

I saw the sudden tensing of her hand and knew that rumour hadn't lied. Agrippinilla, determined to rule, hated the ex-slave who was Claudius's ears and eyes and brain. The man had accompanied the Emperor to Britain and had proved his worth a thousand times. He had been instrumental in revealing the extent of Messalina's wanton behaviour and, since then, had practically run Rome.

To him went the senators seeking favours, the knights wanting to be re-established on the roles, merchants who sought to become Roman citizens. He also guided Claudius in his position of Protector of the Public Morals and had saved many a dissolute youngster from the Emperor's wilful anger. In return he received substantial gifts – in corrupt Rome such traffic was normal.

The programme was a good one and contained a few novelties. Twenty young girls, none over fourteen, were stripped and hung with garlands. They made a pleasant sight as they danced over the sand in time to the music from the band, singing and waving their arms. As the dance ended a score of male chimpanzees were turned loose against them. The animals had been intoxicated on wine laced with cantharides; a potent aphrodisiac made from the dried bodies of a fly found in Spain. The girls too had been daubed with the scent of female apes. Their shrieks as they ran from the rampantly proud animals drowned the music, the crowd laughing and cheering as they were raped and savaged by the beasts.

A few survived the ordeal to be speared together with the chimpanzees by bestiarii dressed in skins and scraps of fur.

Five pairs of myrmillones followed, two of them fighting each other to a standstill and ending their conflict in a stans missus – a draw.

Jugglers followed to fill in the time as slaves hurried to clear the arena of the dead. One of them, a skilful practitioner who kept a stream of coloured balls in the air while he capered and turned beneath them, won the Emperor's favour. He bowed as he was handed a bowl filled with gold pieces.

Beside me Gallus Caecina grunted his contempt.

'Look at that, Atilus. A damned juggler, risking no more than a whipping, gets rich while a decent fighter, chancing his neck, is lucky to get a pittance.'

I took it for a good sign. 'Maybe it's one of his generous days.'

'Claudius doesn't have them. When it comes to handing

out gold he's as tight as a virgin. That juggler must have tickled his fancy.'

Caecina had accompanied the contenders from the school and we stood in the Gate of Death. A good place from which to watch as long as we kept out of the way when the dead were being dragged through.

Some Cretians followed the jugglers, lithe women, naked, their bodies firm, their breasts touched with gold. More gold held back their long hair. Against them were sent bulls, wild creatures with wide-spread horns and flaring nostrils. As they charged the girls gripped the horns and somersaulted over the broad backs. A clever demonstration of athletic skill, but the crowd grew restless at the lack of blood.

It was supplied by bestiarii mounted on horses and armed with lances with which they speared the bulls. The horses were vulnerable and screamed as horns ripped out their intestines. They fell to writhe and kick, an added element of danger to the men who had to dodge the hooves as they fought the bulls.

Several men were gored and tossed into the air like bundles of rag. Others, crushed beneath the falling horses, crawled over the sand with broken legs and shattered knees. Only a few remained unhurt, some, badly injured, groaned as they were dragged past us. One man, gored in the loin, his face smashed from the kick of a horse, screamed as they carried him inside. The screaming stopped with a peculiar squashing sound as of a mallet hitting a melon.

Had he been a gladiator he would have died beneath a charonian's hammer on the sand, but bestiarii had their own ways and customs.

Caecina grunted as he looked at the mess. Blood, guts, droppings of both bulls and horses, pools of urine, all drenched the arena.

I saw Agrippinilla lift a handkerchief to her nose and signal to slaves who set small braziers before her, added incense pluming as it burned to dispel the odours. More slaves ran along the podium, spraying perfume from vases, fanning the air to spread the sweetness. Fine smells for delicate nostrils; for the Emperor, his senators, the Vestal Virgins and other notables who loved the sight of blood but were queasy at its stench.

Flavus helped me to get ready. He was a small, talkative man who had been born a slave and who took care of the armour and shields, polishing them to a brilliant perfection. Now, as he adjusted the straps, he gave me a running commentary.

'The sun's hot, Atilus, so you don't want to mess about too long. Once the sweat starts running into your eyes you'll be at a disadvantage. Remember to keep a firm grip of your sword and be careful of the mess. Now, a little more oil on that shoulder, and you'll be ready.'

'Tighten my belt.'

'It's tight enough,' he insisted. 'You want to be able to breath and move freely.'

'Tighten it.'

'All right, calm down, Atilus. Anything you say. Just calm down.' He fell silent for a moment as he did as I'd ordered. 'A couple of the guards were asking me as to your chances. I told them to bet every denarii they could find on you. If you win they'll give me something and, Atilus, I know that you're going to win. Just get in there and no messing about. The sun—'

'Shut up!' I was tired of his babbling. Flexing my arms I tested the straps, the easy movement of the overlapping plates. The shield fitted snug, but the helmet was a little too large. 'Get some padding.'

He returned with a strip of linen which I bound around my head. The material would soak up sweat as well as making the helmet firm. On the way to the gate through which I would enter the arena I paused before a row of images.

They were stained with time and smoke, the stone greasy, smoothed where touched. Before each stood a bowl containing a few glowing embers.

Taking incense from a box I burned it in honour of Hercules, Nemesis and Mars.

'That's right, Atilus.' Caecina who accompanied me, approved. 'A man is a fool to neglect the gods. Ready now?'

At the gate he handed me my sword.

The sword, the gladius, the short blade with the double edge and keen point. Polished to a brilliant finish, the hilt wrapped with rough threads to provide a good grip, it was the tool with which I would earn my life.

Weapons were the last thing given to a slave-gladiator, the first taken if and when he returned from the arena.

At the sound of the tubae I walked into the sun.

I had done it before, often, but each time was like the first. A few moments to judge the situation, to decide on where to make a stand. A glance upwards to where the awnings or velarium blocked the sun. To the tiers lined with avid faces, some blurred with coloured, shifting shadows from the awnings, others, closer, in sharp detail.

To the man who wanted to kill me.

He was a retiarius, a Nubian, tall, long-limbed, eyes like smoked amber as they watched my every move. The net and trident he held sifted in constant motion, splinters of light flashing from the vicious barbs, the gilded weights edging the mesh. He moved like a cat, light on his bare feet, a proud and successful fighter as the row of silver fish on his broad belt showed; each a proof of victory. A fisherman with a dagger at his belt and death in his heart. Today either he or I would bite the sand.

I moved slowly, taking my time. This was a special bout put on for the benefit of the knowledgeable. There were no trainers to advise us or slaves to lash us on. Proven fighters both we were on our own.

And I was outclassed.

I knew it, could sense it, even smell it as I watched the Nubian edge towards me. As yet I had been lucky, learning as I lived, but now learning was over. I could not rely on his mistakes, his slowness; there was nothing to give me an advantage. Primus had given me added advice, had let me visit Belbrix, and now I knew the reason.

'*Watch*,' the bestiarius had said. '*Watch and know what you're looking for*.'

The tensing of a muscle, the twitch of an eye, the momentary stillness which could preceed action. The shift of a foot, the gleam of sunlight on the barbs of the trident, the weights of the net.

He swirled it, cooing the traditional chant.

'I do not hunt you. I seek a fish. Why do you swim away, Gaul?'

I ignored the words as I did the crowd. Selim was naked but for his belt, his loin cloth, the armour strapped to his left shoulder, a handsome piece embossed with dolphins and crabs. Light flashed from the trident as he moved, questing, the barbs stabbing towards the lattice which protected my face.

The net followed, the mesh aimed at my feet. A common trick, if it wrapped around an ankle I would be pulled off-balance to fall sprawling on the sand. To dodge it was simple, but as I sprang over the net the points of the trident came lancing towards my throat. They caught the upper edge of my shield, the weapon quickly withdrawn as my blade sliced air. Immediately I advanced, shield poised to deflect the thrown net, sword lifting, turning, catching the sunlight and reflecting it back into the amber eyes.

Selim backed, smiling, white teeth flashing in the cavern of his mouth. Skilled, confident, he had anticipated my move. Poised on the balls of his feet he waited for my attack.

'Atilus!' The voice was a lone shout from the upper tiers. 'Get him, Atilus!'

One supporter at least, but there would be more. I had become known and there would be many who had hurried to take advantage of the odds. They, at least, would want me to win.

'Atilus!' yelled the voice again. 'Move in, man! Get him!'

A hint of impatience and I caught the rustle of garments as the crowd stirred, restlessly. Bad signs for a man who might soon need all the popularity he could get. Once down only their mercy could save me and if I put on a bad show that mercy would be withheld. Instead of the flutter of handkerchiefs would come the derisive stabbing of thumbs.

A man, convinced he is outclassed, is beaten before he can begin. I had almost yielded to that weakness, now I dispelled it. The Nubian was a man, nothing more, flesh and blood and a thinking brain. A victor who may have grown overconfident and so a little careless. If he underestimated me that carelessness would grow. When it did my chance would come.

The net came at me and I deflected it – slowly. The trident stabbed and I moved to avoid it, staggering a little as if off balance. My sword cut the air.

And, from the crowd, came jeers.

Selim heard them and paused in his retreat. In the battle between us I was the secutor, the chaser, now he reversed the roles. Advancing he thrust out the trident, caught my blade between the tines and twisted in an effort to trap the weapon. As I tore it free he ran past me, lifting the net as I turned, the mesh a web against the sky as it opened to fall over my helmet.

Dropping to one knee I threw myself sideways, sword cutting at the long, muscular legs, missing as the net had missed. It was drawn back by the thong attached to the Nubian's wrist, the trident darting like a three-tongued asp at the exposed flesh of my back. A move easy to block, but an effective distraction. As I threw up my shield I recognised the feint too late, felt the bite of steel in the flesh of my right thigh.

'Habet!' yelled the crowd. 'He's wounded!'

The skin was torn, the muscle ripped a little, but no serious damage had been done. I could still stand and move even though ruby smears stained my leg and crimson droplets showered on the sand. Panting I regained my feet and backed.

Then Selim made a mistake.

He should have moved straight in, instead he chose to grandstand to the crowd. He moved well clear, clowning, waving the trident, already certain of victory. From the upper tier women screamed open invitations.

'I'm your's tonight, Selim, if you win!'

'Three prongs for him, Selim, one for me!'

'Put him down and ride me until dawn!'

Time for me to think, to plan. A retiarius had to stay clear. In close-quarter combat his exposed body was vulnerable. The trident, dangerous as it was, could not be easily used once a victim was within the range of its shaft. The net was the greatest danger, but that also could not be used to best efficiency on a target too near.

I had to get in close then, to cut and thrust, to down and, maybe, to kill.

I sagged as Selim turned towards me. Not once, despite appearances, had he taken his eyes from where I stood. Now I waited as he edged close, reading his eyes, the movements of his hands. Not yet, the eyes were moving, unsettled. Nor yet, the movements of his hands were wrong. Long hours watching Agonestes had taught me that. In order to throw the net a retiarius had to be in a certain position. There were wide limits of variation, but some things were common. The body used in the cast, the poise of the hand, the feet adjusted to give balance.

Now?

I moved forward, slowly, shield lifted a little, sword moving so as to attract his attention. His eyes shifted, judging distance. Sweat ran over his face and shone wetly on his naked skin.

Now!

I saw the shift of feet, the stillness of the eyes, the gesture of the hand and was running, shield lifted, sword held out from my body, the point upwards. Weights rapped against my shield, the net falling to one side, then I slashed at the trident, caught the shaft, turned the slash into a stab and felt the shock and jar as the blade hit bone.

I hit and stabbed again as I continued my rush, shield now hard against the ebony body, following it as Selim backed, his face strained, eyes wild as he felt the blows.

Minor, all of them. I had hit his bicep and after his ribs. Given time he could have recovered, gained space to put between us, returned to the attack, wiser than before.

I gave him no time. As he dropped the trident and grabbed at my wrist I swung the shield hard against his ribs. He grunted, clawing at his dagger, the net trailing from his wrist. He was so close that I could smell the oil glistening on his body.

'Atilus!'

'Down, you fool! Down!'

'No!'

His grip was iron on my wrist, the sword held back from his body. His dagger rasped on my shield as he tore it from his belt, lifting it to stab at my throat. I slammed up my shield to crack against his elbow and, as the dagger fell from his numbed hand, jerked up my knee between his legs.

As he doubled I stepped back and pushed him down.

'Turn over.'

'What?' He glared at me, clutching his groin, face convulsed with pain.

'Turn over. Lie on your face.'

An enemy should never be underestimated. The traditional pose of the victor standing with his foot on the vanquished's breast makes a fine picture, but a man lying face upwards is still a danger. The Nubian had long arms, his hand could reach up under my kirtle and tear at the genitals.

And he had nothing to lose. He was a missus, a loser, dead if the crowd so decided. The crowd and the Emperor.

I looked to where he sat. Sweat stung my eyes and the lattice blurred my vision. With my sword hand I released the catches and removed the helmet. The crowd roared.

'Atilus! Atilus! Atilus!'

Agrippinilla leaned forward a little, looking at where I stood. Beneath my foot Selim stirred.

'If it goes against me, Atilus, make it quick.'

'It won't.' I had seen the upward thumbs, the flutter of handkerchiefs. Selim was popular, a good fighter. 'You've got a good chance, but it all depends on Claudius.'

He took his time, nodding, frowning, listening as Narcissus spoke in his ear. Then, shrugging, he lifted his thumb.

CHAPTER 15

The latch clicked and I turned, instantly awake, looking at the open door, the dark figure it contained.

'Agonestes?'

'No.' Gallus Caecina stepped into the chamber. 'No Greek love for you tonight, Atilus, if that's your fancy.'

'It isn't.'

'I believe you.' He stood beside the bed, waiting as I rose. 'Here, put this on.'

It was a long cloak fitted with a hood which he pulled over my head and drew close to hide my face.

'You're going on a journey,' he said. 'Not a long one, but someone in the city wants to see you. No names but she's a person of influence. Just do as you're told and you've nothing to worry about. In fact you stand to gain a great deal.' His tone was dryly suggestive.

'A woman?'

'One of your amatori from the arena, I guess. That was a good trick you pulled, baring your face the way you did. Now keep close and make no sound.'

Outside a guard was waiting. He followed me as I walked after Caecina, kept close as we passed through the gate and headed into the city. The streets were busy with carts loaded with sand, grain, wood and other things needed. Some cages held beasts which snarled as men hauled them towards the arena; new animals unloaded at Ostia from ships which had brought them from Africa. Meat for slaughter, during the games the butchers shops held a wide variety of flesh. Some claimed that even the dead men and women were dressed and offered for sale, but that rumour was probably because of the organs removed for the special ashes. The dead, I knew, were buried in deep pits or burned on pyres.

It was late, the stars showing it to be well past midnight, but the streets were far from deserted. Aside from the carts there were pedestrians; artisans busy about their work, women who offered their wares from dark openings. Small bands of men ran down the streets, shouting and waving swords. Sons of the rich, half-drunk and looking for fun. We found an example of their sense of humour.

An old man, stripped naked aside from a loin cloth, cut about the shoulders and arms. He called weakly to us from where he lay in a gutter.

'Help me. Please help me.'

Caecina slowed. 'Trouble?'

'Those hooligans. They robbed me, tore off my clothes and forced me to dance. They cut me with their swords.' He staggered upright and came towards us. His face was bearded, his hair curled in oiled locks.

'Who are you?'

'Ahban ben Jamail. I have a shop at the circus. The best carpets in Rome and I say it without boasting. My house isn't far. If you will help me you won't regret it.'

'A Jew?'

'Yes, but—'

'A Christian?' Caecina spat as the man nodded. 'Then get help from your own, evil kind. I've no time for a man who refuses to honour the gods and to uphold the laws of Rome.'

'I am a loyal citizen. I pay my taxes and obey the laws!'

'And honour our gods?'

'There is only one God.'

'Then ask him for aid. Move, Atilus, we've wasted enough time.'

Twenty yards down the street I asked him about Christians.

'They're rebels.' He was curt. 'The followers of a religious sect with vile practices. They meet in secret places and drink blood and eat flesh. They deny the diety of the God Augustus, the sanctity of the lares and the rule of Rome. Troublemakers the lot of them. One day we'll have to put them in their place.'

'Why? Are they causing harm?'

'They contaminate.' He was still curt. 'I had a good slave once who listened to their lies. It ruined him. He kept telling me that there was a life beyond in which Rome was nothing. That was bad enough while he did his job, but when I found he was persuading others to join the sect I had to take action. Rome is tolerant, but Rome is founded on obedience to law and order. Once that foundation is eroded then who can tell what will happen? Rome is master and the Emperor rules Rome. Simple enough even for a Christian to understand, but they insist there is a higher authority.'

'The slave?'

'Went to the arena.' Caecina sounded vaguely regretful. 'A pity, he was a good worker, but there it is. You can't encourage a thing like that. Well, here we are.'

He halted before a door sunk into a wall in a secluded alley. It was low, barred with metal, a grill set into the surface. Knocking he blinked as light shone into his eyes. A moment and I heard the grate of a bolt on the other side.

As we passed through he said to the guard, 'Wait here and keep watchful.'

A slave had opened the door. He guided us down a narrow path flanked with shrubs which ended at another door set into the wall of a villa. Inside the air was cool and, from somewhere, came the sound of running water.

'For you,' he said looking at me. 'You will bathe and do everything that is ordered.'

I looked at Caecina.

'Do it, Atilus,' he ordered, but was pleased at my deference. 'Just play along.'

Orders from a master were one thing, from a slave another, but those waiting in the chamber holding the bath couldn't be denied.

Three girls waited, all attractive, all wearing only a strip of cotton wrapped around their bodies, the lower edge riding high above their knees, the upper revealing the swell of breasts. Three girls, all mute, the tongues having been torn from their mouths.

With gestures they told me to strip and enter the bath. As I sank into the water they laved my body, scrubbing the skin until it tingled, washed my hair. Dried, combed, scented, the wound in my thigh neatly dressed, they handed me a clean garment. A thin robe which touched the floor and was held at the waist by a cord.

Waiting in a chamber I studied something of the luxury of Rome.

The room was empty of life, but the statues and figures standing against the walls or set into the mosaic floor were company enough. Greek statues robbed from ancient temples, smooth, god-like men, beautiful, serene women. Vases stood around, some filled with flowers, others with pungent herbs, containers of alabaster, jade, amber, striated marble, blown glass in which tiny bubbles caught the light and held it in lambent shimmers. Yellow light from lamps of silver backed by discs of polished bronze.

Chairs of carved wood were softened with cushions embroidered with birds and reptiles. There, a chest which could only have come from Egypt. Here, a table belonging to Judaea. A couch from Syria, soft, inviting, scented with cedar and sandlewood. Carved on a slab of ebony, couples were locked in amorous embraces.

'You like such things, Atilus?'

She had entered the chamber silently, a tall, well-rounded woman, no longer young and yet with a maturity which had added to her attraction instead of diminishing it. One slender, ringed hand made a careless gesture at the ebony slab.

'My husband was interested in such things. A scholar of life, he called himself, but others had a different word for his interests. But you have no cause to worry. He has been dead for three years now and, even if alive, he would not be as jealous as other husbands you have known.'

'Domina?'

'You may call me Flavia, Atilus. A familiar name, is it not? One which must hold for you mixed associations. Tell me, did you enjoy her?'

'Who, Domina?'

'Flavia, who else?' She frowned, tiny creases appearing between her eyes. 'You know who I am talking about. All Rome knows of your association. Were you really both stark naked when Severus caught you?' Her laughter was brittle, artificial. 'What a sight that must have been. No wonder the poor man had a fit.' Seating herself on the couch she ordered, 'Pour me some wine.'

It was dark, rich, the colour of blood, wetting her lips as she sipped at the goblet.

'Talk to me, Atilus. Help yourself to wine and sit at my side. I didn't have you brought here just to stand gawking and silent.' Her hand touched me as I sat, slipping under the robe, her fingers cool against my thigh. 'You were magnificent in the arena today,' she whispered. 'To act as you did, to delude Selim into thinking that he had you, then to attack without hesitation. Sometimes I wish that I could be a man and fight before the crowd. To listen to their cheers. But there are other arenas, Atilus. Smaller but holding as desperate a battle at times.'

'I know.'

'You sound bitter, why? Look at me. Look into my eyes.' They were a pale hazel, large, the whites visible around the irises, the pupils dilated. In them I could see the reflection of my own face. 'We are not talking of the same thing. You are thinking of a woman, a child – your child?'

Of Getia who had fought and lost in the limited world of a bed.

'Domina, why did you send for me?'

'Must you, a man, ask me that?' She came closer and I could smell her perfume. 'Talk to me, Atilus. Excite me with tales of conquest. How do you feel when the blood spurts beneath your sword? When you watch a man die? When you feel the pain of wounds?' Her voice became more urgent. 'And how do you feel when a woman lies beneath you and you enter her? Tell me, Atilus. Tell me!'

The words were hurried, the breath panting, the body close to my own pressing, demanding, but something was wrong. The eyes were too cool, too watchful. This was no spoiled patrician pandering to dissipation.

Why was I here?

Not for sexual play, that I was certain. Or not just for that. She claimed to have seen me fight, but I couldn't remember seeing her and surely a woman of her position would have sat on the podium. And why was she so insistent on my telling her about Flavia?

'Atilus, do as I order!' Her voice was no longer an urgent whisper. 'You realise that I could have you scourged unless you obey? And why hesitate? It is common knowledge how you put the horns on Severus. Just tell me the details.'

'Domina, what details?' I stared at her, meeting her eyes. 'I don't understand. Severus was my master and I was sold as you must know to a lanista.'

'Why?'

The question held the crack of a whip. I remembered the mutes – this woman would have more than a tongue ripped from my body if I aroused her anger.

'How can I answer, Domina? Many slaves were chosen to be sold about that time. I was one of them.'

'You raped your master's wife – or so she claimed, I know better and so do you. Just tell me the details, Atilus, what she said and what happened and then—' Her hand moved higher up my thigh. 'Then, perhaps, you will do the same to me and, when you do, you will receive great rewards. Now tell me, Atilus, and waste no more time. She sent for you, stripped you, offered herself, yes? Answer!'

A woman needing to be titivated – or a woman wanting something else? If she knew of the scandal then why ask for details? A pervert might find pleasure in such a recounting, but this woman was no pervert despite her words. An actress, then, but in that case how had she seen me?

Actresses were low in social standing, almost as low as gladiators who were at the bottom.

I felt a sudden chill, remembering the veiled figures of the Vestal Virgins, the priestesses of Rome. They had stood on the podium – had she been among them?

'Domina!' I sank to my knees before her. 'Whip me if you will, but how can I tell you of things I don't know? What you say didn't happen. I did not rape my master's wife.'

'You swear it?'

'I swear.'

For a long moment she stared down at me and then, with unexpected gentleness ran her fingers through my hair.

'Atilus, rise and finish your wine. One day you must tell me more of the woman I saw in your eyes. Now I shall leave you. Remain here until you are told to go.'

Again I was alone, wondering, mystified. If I had been tested in some way had I passed or failed? What had she really wanted and who had she been? Instinct had dictated my answers to her questions, the caution of an animal which scents a trap, a danger unseen.

I heard a step, a sandal sounding clear on the floor and, turning, saw Macer.

'Atilus!' He moved towards me, right hand extended, the

fingers closing on my wrist as I returned the salutation. 'Man, it's good to see you again!'

He had changed in more ways than one. The eyes were more furtive than I remembered, the cheeks more puffed than his age warranted. He wore the uniform of a tribune of the Praetorian guard.

'You've done well for yourself, Macer.'

'Yes. It helps to know the right people, of course, and the family was an asset. I heard about you being sold but it was too late to do anything about it. Not that I could. Father – what happened, Atilus?'

'A mistake.'

'You can tell me. Flavia was known in Rome and I heard stories. Gossip travels faster than the wind. When I saw that you were listed in the arena and realised that you were the same man I'd known. Well—' He broke off, shrugging. 'The workings of fate, Atilus. A fragment of the past you never expected to see again. Now tell me, what happened back there?'

He was a boyhood companion, a sophisticate, a man who had heard all the scandal and who would appreciate the injustice done to me. Yet, looking into his eyes, I hesitated.

They were strained, watchful like the woman's, the eyes of an interrogator.

'Nothing, Macer,' I said. 'Nothing at all. Flavia persuaded your father to sell off some slaves and I was among them. That's all.'

He relaxed visibly. 'Good. The Emperor is touchy about matters of morals and, if there was talk, well, you understand.'

'There's nothing to talk about, Macer. How is your father?'

'Old and ill but, thank the gods, still alive. Flavia is—' He shrugged. 'Dissatisfied. Gratus is in Rome. He is after a contract to supply beasts to the arena, there's a lot of money in the trade. But you, Atilus, what can we do for you?'

'Get me my freedom.'

'Later, perhaps, even that could be arranged.' His tone was suggestive. 'Now come and join the party.'

It was a subdued affair, a few men and some lanquid women lying on couches and sipping wine as they listened to a young man play a lyre. He was about seventeen, slightly effeminate and expensively dressed. His playing, while accomplished, was far from meriting the applause which greeted the end of his performance.

Macer was in raptures.

'Magnificent! The essence of pure harmony! There isn't an artist in the world who could hope to equal your talent!'

'When you play even the birds fall silent in order to listen,' added a young man with a pimpled face. 'Seneca, you must agree.'

Seneca was about fifty, small, balding, his face thinly scholastic. He said, coldly, 'Many a good artist has been spoiled by too generous an appraisal in his early work. A man of genius is like a flower. He has to be nurtured yet hardened, developed slowly so as to achieve the maximum fullness of bloom. A lesson I have tried to teach and a warning I will continue to repeat.'

'Like a dog howling at the moon.'

'At least I am not whining for a bone, Sulpicus. As Nero's tutor I have a duty both to him and myself. He must be taught the truth undisguised by flattery, I must teach as my conscience demands.'

Nero!

Agrippinilla's son, adopted by the Emperor and now on an equal footing with Britannicus, Messalina's child. If Claudius should die and if the Senate could be swayed to give power to the eldest of the two I was looking at the man who would be the next ruler of Rome.

Suddenly things became clear. Macer's presence and his

concern at the possibility of damaging scandal. As an officer of the Praetorian guard a part of his duties would be to command the men protecting the palace. If Flavia's indiscretions should reach the wrong ears he could lose his position. The mysterious woman, perhaps the High Priestess herself, would have known the truth and kept it hidden for reasons of her own. It was common knowledge that Agrippinilla and Julia were close.

A wrong word, an admission, and I would have been quietly disposed of.

The gods had been kind.

As the lyre began to play again I looked at the young man. His hair was scented, curled, allowed to fall low on his forehead so that he could shake his head to clear his eyes in an affected gesture. Already he was spoiled. The round face was marked with lines of petulance; the attention of his listeners enhanced his self-conceit, the adulation of sychophants reinforced his conviction of superiority.

Against such pressures any tutor would be helpless and Seneca was no exception. He had ridden with the tide, outwardly a firm disciplinarian, secretly encouraging his charge to waste his energies in dissipation. Agrippinilla's work; she needed a man to command the armies and to address the Senate and intended to work through her son once he gained power. Then she, like Augustus's wife Livia, would hold Rome in the hollow of her hand.

CHAPTER 16

I stirred, waking, conscious of the warm impact of naked flesh at my side. I sat up, remembering; the party, the wine, the casual-seeming talk and, later, the female slave who had accompanied me to bed. One of the mutes who had bathed me, soft, willing, more than skilled. A woman who could listen to talk, secrets, even plots, but who could never betray those who had spoken.

Smiling she touched my face.

Later, after I had bathed and eaten and dressed in new and expensive clothes, Gallus Caecina came to see me.

'Well, Atilus, you passed. Nero likes you and so does your hostess.'

'Julia?'

He frowned and shook his head. 'No names, Atilus. What you don't know can't hurt you. Just do as you're told and you won't regret it.'

He was old, steeped in caution, playing a desperate game and I could understand his reluctance. But some things I had learned from words spoken the previous night. A name, an intention, a concern.

Julia, the High Priestess of Rome, owned the villa. Nero, young, impulsive, the potential Emperor, needed to be guarded. I had attracted the attention of Agrippinilla and she had noted my youth and skill.

I was to be the young man's bodyguard.

An imperial slave to guard the heir to Rome.

Caecina explained, labouring the point. 'You're young, Atilus, and Nero likes to be surrounded by young men. You know how to hold your tongue and Macer has recommended you. You've no other patrons and haven't become involved with any of the patricians. I think it's a good choice and if you're smart you'll make the most of the opportunity.' His voice became suddenly hard. 'But if you fail, Atilus – you'll die on a cross!'

A threat which had always been present, but one which diminished as I took up my new life.

The duties were simple, to be always on hand when Nero needed me, to sleep when I could, eat before he did, listen to him when he wanted to expound his views.

'Music is the highest of the arts, Atilus, don't you agree? Only when composing can a man approach the joy experienced by the gods. A poem holds within itself the distilled essence of all wisdom, a song the emotions of a lifetime. Listen to this and tell me what you think.'

Knowing he liked praise I gave it to him, yet not all of it was undeserved. Had his life been different, had he been allowed to grow in a normal manner, he would have made a good actor and a fair musician. His talent, though lacking self-criticism, was real. The skill he could have developed had been stunted by his sycophants.

And he had unexpected depths of compassion.

'Look, Atilus.' A bird, a present from an eastern prince, had died. Nero cradled it in his hands, tears streaming down his cheeks. 'Such a little thing and it sang so sweetly. Why did it have to die? Were the gods jealous of the music it made? Why is life so cruel at times?'

I said, 'All things are born to die, Nero. The bird, at least, was saved from the pain of old age.'

'You are right, my friend.' My answer had pleased him. 'The gods were kind, not cruel.' He threw aside the limp bundle of flesh and feather. 'Sulpicus is giving a party and I mustn't be late.'

The pimpled young man was the scion of a powerful family; Agrippinilla was careful in her choice of friends for Nero. His villa was blazing with light as we approached, men dressed as beasts standing on guard, bears, lions, apes, the skins real, the claws and fangs gilded.

Inside music echoed through the chambers and near-naked women laughed as they ran from men wearing the masks of satyrs. Wine flowed freely, served by seductive slaves, their hair gilded, breasts exposed, nipples painted a bright scarlet. Smiling they stood patient beneath questing hands.

'A song, Nero!' Sulpicus, more than a little drunk, reared up from his couch. 'Play for us and turn the night into melody. The touch of your hand on a lyre and magic comes to reign.'

'Not tonight.' Nero was firm. 'The muse is not with me.'

'Impossible, you and the muse are one.' Italicus, not to be outdone in his adulation, lifted both hands towards the ceiling. 'Death would come as a friend if accompanied by one of your poems.'

Nero's eyes flickered as if he had been struck by a sudden idea. Before he could voice it a slave offered wine. I took the goblet, tasted it, found it innocuous and handed it to Nero. With sudden petulance he threw it down.

'Am I to be given no peace? Always you demand that I give freely of my art. Can none of you understand that an artist is a creature of inspiration?' He waved aside the babble of protest. 'Sulpicus, you promised me entertainment. Am I a beggar to play for my supper?'

'Nero! Master! I am dirt at your feet!'

'Yes, you are, aren't you.' Nero looked at the grovelling figure. 'Then, as you are dirt, I shall tread on you.' He did so, smiling as Sulpicus grunted beneath his weight. 'Atilus, join me.'

I added my weight to his own.

'Thrasea, Vibius, Decimus – all of you, come and join me.'

Weight enough to have crushed the unfortunate man's ribs, to have driven the shattered bone into his lungs. I stepped from him as others ran forward.

'If you kill him, Domini, he won't be able to provide the promised entertainment.'

'That's true, Atilus. Again you show your wisdom. Rise, dirt, and act the host. Your guests grow impatient.'

Some dancers ran out into the open space between the tables and couches, lithe young women from Alexandria, learned in the eastern arts. Music rose as they moved in writhing abandon, each gesture an invitation, hips, buttocks and breasts thrusting, circling, fluid with liquid grace.

Bored, Nero toyed with a pomegranate, spitting out the seeds.

A troupe of acrobats came next, midgets who spun and twisted in the air, landing like cats to turn cartwheels, to walk on their hands, to balance balls on their feet. Dressed in gaudy colours they looked like tiny parodies of men, boys with ancient faces.

Nero yawned. 'Is this all you have to show me, Sulpicus? I had hoped for something better. As Seneca is always telling me, an artist needs the creative impulse of novelty. This.' His hand drifted towards the acrobats, 'is hardly the material for an epic. You disappoint me.'

'A moment, muse of the world!' Sulpicus waved dismissal at the troupe. 'The best is reserved for the last. Behold!'

A pair of dimachaeri ran into the open space as he clapped his hands.

Both were young, both naked, both holding a pair of matched daggers in their hands. Oil gleamed on their bodies and their hair was held back by a fillet of gold. Twin brothers, I guessed from the look of them. Slaves, privately trained, used to provide entertainment at parties such as this. Expensive entertainment, such fighters didn't come cheap.

I looked at them with professional interest as they bowed to the assembly. Thin scars marred the oiled perfection of their bodies, the marks of previous combats, yet they seemed too young to have had many. Trained young, then, fighting as mere boys. Dimachaeri were not often seen in the arenas of Rome, their skill was too delicate to be appreciated by the mob, but they were popular with the experts.

'Pollux and Castor,' said Sulpicus. 'To first, second or third blood, Nero. The choice is yours.'

'To the death.'

Sulpicus bit his lip as the fighters stiffened and I knew that his arrangement hadn't included such a termination. His concern was financial, if he obeyed Nero the cost would be high.

'Death?' His laugh was brittle. 'Surely not, master of all art? You, more than any, can appreciate the deft touch, the symbolical ending. Alive they will portray the symphony of motion, dead they are only food for the dogs.'

'To the death,' insisted Nero. He raised himself on his couch, lips full, eyes reflecting an inner hunger. 'Let them fight and let them die. To the winner I will give a circle of gold.' He pulled a bracelet from his arm. 'Let them fight, Sulpicus. Now!'

The music stilled as the fighters turned to face each other hands lifting, daggers poised. They held the weapons sword-fashion, thumbs to the blade, the points tilted upwards. A grip enabling them to both cut and stab, to block and parry.

Made of tempered steel, each blade almost a foot long, they made a clear ringing sound as they touched. A sound like bells, the chiming of a sistrum, gladiator's music.

I watched as they began their dance of death.

Pollux was to my left, he moved, left dagger extended, the right drawn back, a pose adopted by his twin. For moments they weaved, feet gliding over the inlaid floor and, watching, I began to sense how each would act.

Castor would feint with his left, slice at the arm while his right dagger caught and held the opposed weapon. Pollux would engage, withdraw, attempt a cut across the other's chest.

For a moment there was a flurry of movement, the ring of blades, the harsh breathing of struggling men. A performance in which neither was hurt. A rehearsed act to impress those watching.

'Twenty gold pieces on Castor,' said Italicus. 'Am I taken?'

'Taken.' Vibius made a note on a tablet. 'Nero?'

He glanced at me, eyebrows lifted, wanting my advice. I hesitated before giving it, the pair were too evenly matched, but it was to the death and one had to win. Pollux, from what I could see, was a trifle faster, less easy to read.

'Atilus?'

'Pollux.'

'Fifty pieces on Pollux,' said Nero. He sucked in his breath as a knife struck home.

Castor had won first blood, his blade cutting a crimson gash over his brother's chest, a thin, shallow wound which dripped an ooze or carmine. His own wound came shortly after, a cut on the inside of his left arm, not deep enough to sever the tendons. Breaking they paused for a moment, looking at each other, then as one, they resumed the contest.

I could appreciate their skill. Swords were relatively heavy, slow, a swing taking time to develop and turn. The daggers were light, thin, vicious blades with honed edges and needle points. They darted like the tongues of serpents cutting, always cutting, crossing oiled skin with a mesh of crimson lines, gashes which joined in a web of lacerated flesh.

The sica of a Thracian produced much the same result, the curved edge designed to slice rather than thrust. The advantage they had when facing a retiarius, the blade against the net severing the mesh instead of knocking it aside as happened with a gladius. But Thracians carried a shield, wore a helmet, a greave. These dimachaeri had nothing. Nothing but their knives.

Their panting was real now, the blood dappling the tiles smearing beneath their feet, staining their toes, their heels. Yet, while cut, both were still relatively uninjured. The shallow gashes would smart, but would heal quickly given time.

But, for one of them, there would be no time. This fight was to the death.

Pollux was the first to fully realise it as I had guessed he would. Trained together, living together, the product of the same womb, they had a natural reluctance to kill or even to seriously hurt each other. They fought to provide a spectacle, a display of skill for the knowledgable who demanded techniques rather than simple killing. They had never known the arena, heard the howl of the mob, only the villas and palaces of the rich, the comments of the cultured.

'In!' Nero was shouting, his face flushed, eyes avid. 'In, Pollux! In!'

'Castor!' A man yelled the name, yielding to the moment. 'Cut him, Castor.'

More voices joined the others, women, more calculating than the men, screaming for Nero's choice.

He heard and responded, daggers flashing, winking as they reflected the light, the edges dulled with ugly stains. Castor staggered, the dagger falling from his right hand, a fountain of blood gushing from the inside of his wrist. As Pollux came forward he raised his left hand and thrust at his brother. The point hit the chest, grated on a rib, tore open the side of the torso.

A mistake, a knife-fighter rarely stabbed, to do so was to risk trapping the blade and always, unless he was fast, the move left him open.

Pollux swung up his right arm, knocked aside the blade, moved in and slashed his own across the other's stomach.

Castor looked down. The cut had been deep, the muscles

severed, the bulge of intestines clearly visible. He gripped them with his good hand, blood pouring over his fingers as, practically disembowelled, he looked at his brother.

'Pollux! As you love the gods – please!'

A prayer answered with a dagger thrust into his heart.

Nero chuckled as he fell.

'Magnificent! A perfect ending! Sulpicus, I must congratulate you – you have provided me with the raw material for a tragedy in the Grecian style. The love of a man for his brother, sending him to the gods to end his pain, remaining to mourn his passing. Superb!'

CHAPTER 17

The days slid into weeks. There were more parties; assemblies at which men gathered to speak in low voices, others which degenerated into scenes of wild abandon. At such times I was hard put to it to be diplomatic; a rejected woman can be a dangerous animal, but it was impossible to give them all what they demanded. My duty to Nero came first – a matter of survival, not of inclination. The list of qualifications Gallus Caecina had credited me with had omitted one particular. I was expendable and I knew it. So I smiled at Nero's jests, stayed firmly by his side and acted in all ways to give satisfaction. At times it wasn't easy.

Often he would gather a group of friends together with their attendant gladiators and go racing through the city at night looking for fun. Sometimes it consisted of beating up helpless wayfarers especially if they happened to be Jews. There were fights with other gangs of hooligans and, when that palled, he would head into the slums, burst into the tenements and fondle the women while threatening the men. Sometimes he did more than fondle, urged on by his companions and laughing as they took their turn.

Once, when an outraged father came at him with a stave, only my quick action prevented Nero from joining his father in hades.

As way of thanks he took me to visit Acte.

She was a Greek freedwoman, very lovely, and Nero had established her in a house secluded at the edge of the fashionable quarter. The money for this had been obtained from friends, among them Serenus who, officially, had Acte under his protection. A transparent device to keep Agrippinilla from knowing of the girl and her influence.

Nero was proud of her. As he introduced me he said, 'Well, Atilus, don't you think she is the most beautiful woman you have ever seen?'

'Atilus?' She spoke before I could answer. 'The gladiator?'

'My bodyguard, Acte.'

'But a gladiator and a slave!'

Nero was stubborn. 'He is what I say he is and he saved my life. Be kind to him, Acte. I order you to be kind.'

She smiled and held out her hands for me to touch. A few years older than Nero she was far wiser and, as he had ordered, she was kind. A natural response, I think, she too had once been a slave, and a thing like that is never forgotten. Yet I could sense her dilemma. To be too kind was to invite his jealousy, to defy his wish was to earn his anger.

Skilfully she chose the middle path.

'I am glad to receive any man who has saved the life of Nero.'

'I am honoured to be presented to such a beautiful woman, Domina.' Pausing I added, 'But my master is pleased to exaggerate. I did him some small service, that is all.'

'Small?' He frowned, then chuckled. 'You have a sense of humour, Atilus. Don't listen to him, Acte. He did what I said.'

'Then you must remember it, Nero. If there comes a time when you can do something for him in return it would be generous to do so.'

He caught her meaning. 'He is an imperial slave, Acte, not mine. I cannot free him.'

'But if you could?'

'Then he would be as free as any man in Rome. I swear it.'

'Before the lares?' Smiling she led him to where the household gods stood in a row against the wall. They were small, beautifully carved, the incense she burned before them sweetly pungent. 'You see, my dear, I swear eternal feality to you. My heart, my life, my spirit to be yours now and for always. This I swear.'

'And I also.' Nero threw powder into the embers.

'And Atilus?' She urged him, her voice gentle. 'A small thing for so great a deed, my dear. And, in the future, who can tell what friends you may need?' Her voice dropped to a whisper as she murmured something in his ear.

'Yes, Acte, as always you are right.' Smoke rose as he burned incense before the lares. 'Before the gods, Atilus, I swear to give you your freedom when I am able.'

A promise wrung from a stimulated boy – how could I rely on it if and when it fell within his power to grant my dearest wish? Yet it was better than nothing and, at least, Acte had proved herself to be a friend.

I thought of her as I stood guard in the chamber next to the one into which she had taken him. The door was thin, no barrier to the sighs, whispers, groans and sounds of hectic movement.

Acte's maid, a small, slender girl with a badly scarred cheek which she did her best to hide beneath the mane of her hair, paused in her passage across the room.

'So Nero is riding again tonight,' she said. 'Well, there are worse things he could do.'

I saw the movement of her hand towards the scar.

'Nero?'

'I was crimping my lady's hair when he flew into a fit of anger. The curling irons were heating in a brazier and he snatched them and held them to my face.'

'Why?'

'He said that I smiled. May the gods help Rome if smiling becomes a crime. But he was mistaken. I was afraid, he looked like an animal, and I was going to scream for help. If I had he would have burned out my eyes.'

'That boy?'

'That devil. Don't you know him yet? Well, you will if you live long enough. He's mad. Insane.'

A woman vengeful for her lost beauty, naturally she would exaggerate, yet already I sensed that she held the truth. Little things had altered my first opinion. An artist, yes, but a warped one who took pleasure in things which normal men thought vile. One who, guided by Seneca, was already testing the boundaries of human tolerance.

But that was not my concern. Nero could destroy Rome for all I cared and I would help him – as long as first he gave me my freedom.

It was late when we left the house. A wisp of crescent moon hung low on the horizon and the air held the peculiar stillness which heralds the approach of dawn. In the distance a dog barked, the sound clear, taken up and repeated by other canine guardians. As they fell silent Nero pointed at the sky.

'Look, Atilus. A comet.'

His eyes were as sharp as my own. The thing was barely visible among the cold glitter of stars.

'An omen,' he mused. 'Such things presage great events. One was seen just before Julius Caesar was assassinated and another foretold the destruction of Carthage. A sign from the gods, Atilus. If I were Claudius I would not sleep well at night.'

The Emperor rarely did. I had heard tales of how he woke, crying out as he gripped his stomach, needing draughts of warmed wine laced with opium to give him rest. An internal complaint for which his Greek physicians suggested and prescribed hot tiles to be laid on his paunch together with enemas and purges. Fearing poison he ate only fresh fruit and vegetables.

Nero hummed softly to himself as we walked down the path leading from the house. It was narrow, flanked with laurel, a smouldering torch set in a cresset above the door doing little to dispel the shadows. As we rounded a curve, I slowed, listening. There was no wind and yet the leaves had rustled.

Nero bumped into me as I halted.

'Atilus—'

'Get behind me, Domini!'

The rustle had been close and high, the sound a man would make if he eased his way through the bushes. It came from my left and something, a blur, moved on the path ahead. A sword was belted at my waist and I drew it. As it cleared the scabbard the men attacked.

There were two of them, faces masked, swords naked in their hands. One came running up the path directly towards me, the other, shoving his way through the laurel, had hoped to hit from behind, a plan now ruined by his careless movement.

I backed, pressing Nero behind me into the laurel, blocking the sword swung by the man on the path and thrusting in turn, the short, vicious stab beloved of the legions. He gasped, clutching at his side, blood showing dark between the fingers as he backed beyond reach. I could have followed but his companion was close and Nero had caught hold of my belt, hampering my mobility.

'Atilus! Protect me!'

Metal rang as the blades touched, grated as they slid one over the other, rang again as, beating the other's weapon aside, I brought up my sword in a sweeping, back-handed slash which dragged the edge over the masked face.

A blow which would have killed had he not swayed back in time. He groaned, hand clutching at the mask, the sudden rush of blood and then, as I advanced, he turned and was gone, racing down the path after his companion.

'Atilus!' Nero, his fear conquered now that the danger was past, trembled with anger. 'Chase them. I must know who sent them to kill me.'

'No, Domini. There could be others.'

For a moment it seemed that he would insist, then he nodded, gnawing at his bottom lip.

'You are right, Atilus. And there is no need. Claudius hates me. He wants to hand the purple on to Britannicus when he dies. If I should be killed then the Senate would have no choice but to make him Emperor. It's obvious who must have sent those men.'

He was young and shrewd, but not shrewd enough. The men had run too fast to have been tools of the Emperor. I remembered the slave with the scarred face and thought it more than possible that she had hired the bravos, paying them with gifts received from her mistress, but I kept silent. Betraying her would gain me nothing and I could be wrong. Outraged husbands also had good reason for wanting Nero dead.

The next day I was summoned into the private chamber.

Julia used many names and liked to watch from secret places and she had a habit of sitting, thickly veiled, in the cool shadows of her inner room when she would question the wives of senators about their indiscretions.

As the High Priestess of the Vestal Virgins she had the religious welfare of the city under her control; a strong position which gave her the power to insist that Claudius banish offenders from the city or even from Italy itself. The wives, always fearful, were ready to confess all. The knowledge gave her an advantage which she used when the necessity arose.

But the woman waiting for me, veiled in white, was not Julia.

I knew it as I knelt, noting little things, the naked feet, the perfume, the crest of hair beneath the folds of lace. Julia, conscious of her ugly toes, never wore open sandals. She scented her body with floral odours, not the heavier unguents from the east. Her hair was thinner, worn close about her head.

This woman could only be Agrippinilla.

When she spoke her voice was muffled, disguised by an olive which she held in her mouth.

'Atilus, Nero owes you much and he recognises the debt. He will not forget to repay you, but you must be patient. Soon, all will be as you wish. Do you understand?'

My freedom, if not actually promised at least implied, and I wondered if she knew of the oath he had made. It seemed unlikely, Acte would have said nothing and would have taken precautions against spies. Nero himself, then, but no, he would not have wanted to mention his meeting with the girl.

A bribe, then, but why?

The reason became obvious as she continued. 'Tonight you are to undertake a special task. You are not to be seen either going or returning. You will avoid the city watch and you will do exactly as I say, no more and no less.'

'My duties with Nero?'

'Are suspended. He is to leave on a visit to friends in Campania. Now listen closely to what you must do.'

It was dark when, muffled in a cloak, I left the villa in search of Locusta. She was to be found in a small house set close to the Tiber, a place stained with a pattern of lichen, a phallus daubed in red to the right of the door.

Inside the air was dank and chill, the cloying odour of incense doing little to mask the stench of bad meat and rancid oil. Shadows dulled the corners of the room and the eyes of rats peered from the gloom. The woman who let me in was old, stooped, her back hunched and her eyes milky with cataracts.

She grunted as she peered at the coin I placed in her hand and, without another word, led me up the stairs and ushered me into a small chamber lit by a single lamp.

In its light a woman sat behind a small table on which rested an assortment of phials, dried pieces of skin, some fragments of bone and a skull.

'Locusta?'

'I am she.'

With an effort I masked my surprise. I had expected to meet a crone, instead I looked at a woman of about middle-age, her face pale beneath coiled tresses of ebony hair. Her cheeks were hollowed, the lips thin and bloodless, her eyes the colour of grain which has been left to bleach in the sun.

Her voice was like the rattle of dusty leaves.

'You have come for what? A love philtre to win the heart and body of a woman who has aroused your desire?'

'No.'

'A potion, then, to kill a life you have unwisely planted in an unsuitable womb?'

'No.'

'Then surely a draught to give you strength; to stiffen your sword so as to gain advancement and pleasure in the arena of love?'

'No.'

Three refusals as my orders had specified. 'I need your help and for it I offer you this.'

She made no comment as I dropped the half of a broken coin into her palm. Turning she did something which I could not see, but guessed she was comparing it with another. The pieces must have fit for, without a word, she handed me a small phial.

'Is this all?'

The inclination of her head cast a shadow on the wall, black, monstrous, like a warning. Locusta was a woman rumoured to be skilled in the manufacture of poison – what had she given me?

I studied it on the way back, standing beneath a torch set at a cross-street. The phial was made of porphyry, the stopper sealed with black wax traced with the outline of a skull. A small thing to contain the power of death but I was certain that it lay inside, in a liquid which, added to wine, would kill as surely as a sword.

I left it where I had been directed, on a small table in the garden, a squared slab from which birds pecked scattered crumbs.

The next morning I was returned to the school.

The following week Claudius died.

CHAPTER 18

Agonestes brought the news. He had been taken up by a rich senator who showered him with presents in return for the use of his body and had made certain arrangements with those who ran the school. The Greek was near the end of his sentence and would not fight again in the arena unless he chose. Soon he would be free to live as he wished.

Free!

The gladius in my hand smashed against the post and chopped straw flew as if beaten by a flail.

Life with Nero had made me soft. There had been too much wine, good food, lack of exercise. Too many complaisant women who had demanded that I ease the ache of their loins. Policy dictated that I satisfy their demands if I was to retain their friendship. Denied they would have made vicious enemies.

'You've heard that Claudius is dead, Atilus?'

'Yes.'

More straw flew as I swung the sword. Sweat sheened my body and ran into my eyes, blurring my vision so that the post became a man, balding, weak-legged, grotesque in his regalia. Claudius who had conquered my people, whose soldiers had raped and killed my mother.

Mushrooms had killed him so the rumours had said. A dish of fresh mushrooms one larger, more tempting than the others. Agrippinilla had eaten from the same dish, leaving the best for the Emperor. Eating he had fallen into convulsions and quickly died.

'But have you heard the rest?' Agonestes stepped closer. 'The Praetorians have proclaimed Nero as the new Emperor. The Senate has bowed to their demands and accepted him.

Bribery, of course, Nero shared a fortune between the officers and men and has promised more.'

Nero the Emperor?

The sword froze in my hand. 'Agonestes, are you certain?'

'I had it from Paccius.'

His patron who would know the truth behind rumour.

Agrippinilla had been cunning. Not only had she won the support of the Praetorians but she had also arranged for Nero to marry Octavia, Claudius's daughter and so enhance her son's claims. The marriage-promise had won over reluctant senators. Britannicus had been pushed aside and my recent charge was now the ruler of Rome.

And he had sworn an oath before the gods to free me when he was able.

'Atilus!' Agonestes gripped my arm. 'Are you well?'

'Yes.'

'Your face! You looked as if you'd seen a vision. The sun,' he decided. 'You've been over-doing the exercises.'

'I'm all right.'

'Well, you should know.' His hand touched my arm, the fingers caressing. 'Take care of yourself, my friend. I have a regard for you as you are aware. Soon, perhaps, something may be done.'

'I want only my freedom.'

'Yes, I know, and I've mentioned it to Paccius. I have to be careful, he's a very jealous man, but he has influence. I promise nothing, Atilus, but rest assured that you have friends.'

Smiling I returned the grip of his hand. Agonestes meant well and he couldn't know that I was as good as free. Soon now, surely, Nero would remember his oath.

A hope which faded as the days passed. Great things were happening in Rome, but they washed over the school like the wind over waves, leaving no trace of passing. Men, previously banished, were returning to the city. Families which had been in disgrace now bloomed in favour. Crimes against the state were forgiven to those who had won the Emperor's ear. Many of Claudius's decrees were abolished and a holiday atmosphere pervaded the city.

And still I waited.

Agrippinilla could not have forgotten her implied bribe even if her son was too busy to remember me. Impatient I toyed with the idea of bringing pressure to bear. Paccius, primed by Agonestes, could carry the word. A hint that, unless I was freed, questions would be raised about a certain container obtained from a woman known to have skill in the manufacture of poison.

Poison which could have been sprinkled on the mushroom Claudius had eaten – and who else could have done it but Agrippinilla?

With a shock I realised I had no proof.

The house had been a low-class brothel, abandoned, used for the one occasion. The woman who had admitted me had been almost blind and could never identify the man who had arrived in darkness nor the woman who had waited in the upper chamber. Locusta would deny everything and had probably arranged for others to swear she was elsewhere at the time. Agrippinilla had been disguised and thus unseen.

It would be my word against hers – and I was a slave.

There was nothing I could do.

Grimly I concentrated on the exercises, rebuilding muscle and stamina, working until the heavy practice-sword felt like a wand, the shield a scrap of parchment. If one road to freedom had closed then the other still remained open. To fight and win and to earn the rudis. To kill and climb to liberty on the bodies of the dead.

One night Gallus Caecina came to visit me in my room. He was wearing a dark cloak and came unaccompanied and I reared as I saw him, tense and ready for battle, relaxing only when he spoke.

'It's me, Atilus.'

'Word from the Emperor?'

'In a way.' He sat on the edge of the bed, his voice so low that I had to lean towards him and strain to catch the words. 'I've been given instructions to put you into the arena.'

He made no comment at my assumption that Nero had taken a personal interest in me and I guessed that he knew or suspected more than he was willing to admit.

'A big munera has been arranged to celebrate the Emperor's marriage to Octavia. The best of gladiators have been obtained and a point was made that you should be matched against a certain opponent. The chances—' He broke off then said, abruptly, 'I like you, Atilus, and I think you've earned more than you're getting. I'll do my best but the rest is up to you. Do you understand?'

He was trying to tell me something, but I couldn't guess what. A warning? But what need was there of that? I would fight and win if I could and, maybe, Nero would grant me the rudis.

The rudis!

I drew in my breath as I realised what could be intended. The Emperor, guided by his mother, would be reluctant to free a slave, a gladiator, without apparent cause. There would be gossip and those who suspected that Claudius had been poisoned would be alert for any sign. Caution would dictate discretion, but no one would think it odd that a gladiator should be given the rudis.

And Nero would have kept his word.

The cunning and the guile of Rome – the full extent of which I had yet to experience.

Things were not normal. I was not allowed to join the others at the customary feast held at the eve of the munera,

Primus insisting that I needed further training. I ate alone and was kept in isolation, more proof that something was in the wind. And when I was due to fight I was hurried to the arena in a closed sedan.

It was the old amphitheatre built by Titus Statilius Taurus and was made partly of stone and the rest of wood. The preparation rooms were small and cramped, over-crowded now with the throngs of gladiators, trainers, attendant slaves. Under the direction of Gallus Caecina I was hastily prepared, the helmet with its masking lattice the first item of equipment to be fitted. Flavus, the slave who usually attended me, was nowhere to be seen.

I was alone, unrecognised, unknown.

As we moved towards the row of gods for me to make the customary offering Caecina whispered, 'Atilus, you remember what you did the last time you fought? Well, bear it in mind.'

A hint? If so I couldn't understand what he was getting at. Everything was abnormal, the preparation, the obvious intention to keep me from sight, all made no sense. If they had wanted to kill me then why not poison in my barley or a dagger thrust in the night?

But why should anyone want me dead?

As we reached the opening of the Gate of Life the tubae sounded, clear notes echoing to the sky. The podium was thick with dignitaries; ambassadors, prefects, consols, the Vestal Virgins, the Emperor himself.

Nero was wearing purple, his red hair curled and oiled, touches of rouge on his cheeks. Rings weighed his hands and a naked slave boy crouched at his feet holding a lyre. Octavia, his wife, sat at his right, a slip of a girl looking little more than a child. On his left Agrippinilla dominated the scene with her presence.

On the sand, waiting, stood Selim.

No one shouted as I walked towards him, turning to lift

my gladius in salute to the royal party, and that was strange.

Always before, since I had shown my worth, my amatores in the tiers would yell and shout encouragement. Every proven gladiator had his followers and I was no tiro fresh from the school, but a tried and tested spectati. The only reason for their silence was that they couldn't have known who I was.

As Nero couldn't have known.

But Agrippinilla did.

I knew it as I knew my own name and knew too why things had been handled as they had. An accomplice would have been needed to ensure my death – and why should the mother of the Emperor want a slave to die? This way there could be no questions. I would fight and I would be killed and my mouth would be closed for eternity.

And Selim would do the killing.

A perfect choice, I had beaten him once and he had been lucky to escape with his life. A thing he would not forget. His pride and standing had been hurt and I had been the cause.

He sneered as he uttered the traditional chant.

'I do not hunt you. I seek a fish. Why do you swim away – Atilus?'

The name was spoken almost in a whisper, but loud enough to tell me that he knew who I was, to tell me also that I could hope for no mercy. He would down me and kill me before the crowd could give their verdict.

The lash of the net was like the barb of his tongue.

I dodged it easily, standing poised on the balls of my feet, moving as the mesh fell to catch the thrust of the trident on my sword. Preliminary touches as we circled each other, Selim standing well clear. Not again would he be deluded into underestimating me. This time he wouldn't fall victim to a sudden rush which would carry me within the range of his weapons.

I edged close, cut, withdrew, feeling the sting of weights

on my naked back. The trident darted at my eyes but I wasted no effort in beating it aside. The lattice I wore would protect them.

The lattice which helped to even the odds between a retiarius and a secutor. The lash of a weight in an eye and the combat would be as good as over. The barbs of the trident thrusting at the naked face would engage the full attention of an opponent and make him vulnerable to the cast of the net. The heavy shield would slow him down. The gladius with its straight blade was designed to thrust and chop, not to slash. The careful balancing of armour and weapons which made our combat an almost even dance of death.

Almost – but Selim held the advantage.

He moved like oil, graceful, body gleaming in the sun. I caught the flash from his armour, the lift of his left shoulder, saw the gleam of barbs and swung my sword as they came up to thrust at my neck. The edge slammed against the shaft and I weaved, the thrown net hitting my shield, the trident stabbing again at my exposed side.

Net and barbs working in harmony, opposed by shield and sword and rapid movement.

'Selim! Selim! Selim!'

The crowd yelled as he cast his net, the mesh opening, falling, jerked to one side by the thong attached to his wrist. It touched my helmet and settled over my shield tightening as he pulled.

I turned to my right, the gladius sweeping up and over, the edge drawn back as it touched the strands. A sica would have cut through it, the gladius did little more than fray the mesh, lift it up and throw it to one side.

The trident came at me, the barbs aimed for my thigh, clashing as they hit my upraised greave.

A move which left him open, but standing on one foot I could get little power into the blow without losing my balance. Even so it would have cut his arm to the bone had he not lunged forward to take it on the galerus.

I spun as he passed me to run clear, to stand, panting, as he faced me.

'You are fast, Atilus,' he said. 'Faster than you were, but still not good enough to beat me. Yield now and I promise you a quick ending.'

Talk to gain time, to distract attention as he readied his net.

'Just then you almost fell. Luck alone saved you. How long can it last? It is only a matter of time before you bite the sand.'

A veterani talking from conviction. Down I would add another silver ornament to his belt.

Another life to Rome.

The anger came, closing out the world, leaving nothing but the retiarius. A beast who intended to kill me, an animal to be studied.

Training would have given him certain reflexes, actions taken without the need for deliberate thought. A system which had proved its worth in previous bouts as his continued existence proved. He would rely on them, use them – how to turn them against him?

How to get in close so the sword could cut and stab flesh instead of air?

I moved, noted his reaction, backed to advance again and make the same move, seeing the same response. The trident lifted to block the sword as my own shield rose to block the net. I exaggerated the movement, lifting it higher each time, tilting it up and away from my body to expose the naked flesh beneath.

Three times, five – on the seventh he lunged.

I was ready and waiting. As the barbs stabbed at my torso I swayed to my right, felt the shock and burn of steel and then was moving forward, the gladius a glitter as it flashed in the sun, the edge falling towards his head, his face.

A blow aimed to split the skull, missing as he threw himself backwards, the point cutting down his cheek, opening his chest in a long, shallow gash.

'Habet!' The crowd yelled as he backed, sand pluming beneath his naked feet. The sound changed, became wild as I followed. 'Verbera! Verbera!'

Strike! Strike! Smash the sword on the skull, the arm, the body. Bury the edge, the point, let blood flow like a fountain, gushing, pulsing, staining the sand!

Kill! Kill!

The demand of Rome – the law of the arena!

Selim turned, taking a slash across the back as he raced over the sand. A burst of energy which carried him beyond my reach and gave him time to regain his stance. He edged towards me, no longer smiling, not as confident as he had been, but just as determined to win.

A determination matched by my own.

The barbs had torn the flesh of my side, blood running from the wound stained my greave. Selim's own wounds gave him a striated appearance, the opened cheek ruining his coldly handsome face. A face which snarled as he gripped the trident in both hands, holding it as he would a spear, using the power of both arms as he slammed it towards my face.

I felt the jar as the barbs hit my lowered helmet, the upper rim of my shield. Powerful thrusts which would tear through the lattice and put out my eyes should they land. The gladius was too short to reach him and he stayed well away, holding the trident at its full extent. All I could do was to attempt to divert his thrusts, to knock aside the tines and lunge forward within its reach.

Twice I tried – the third time he trapped my blade.

It was luck, but he did not hesitate. As the blade slipped

between the tines he twisted, catching the sword and tearing it from my hand to spin and fall hilt upward, the point buried in the sand.

'Now, Atilus,' he gloated. 'You die!'

Rigid thinking instilled over the years and verified by many combats. Thinking which made him a little slow to claim his victory.

I made an apparent attempt to run to the sword and he moved in front of it. Time enough for me to rip the shield from my arm and to send it spinning, edge on, towards his face. As he ducked I ran forward, grabbed the end of the net and pulled.

Trapped by the thong about his wrist he staggered after me, snatching at the trident with his left hand. I gave him no chance to use it. Feet straddled I swung the net in a circle, pulling him after it, using him as if he were a weight attached to the end of a line. Intent on retaining his feet he flung aside the trident, snatched at his dagger and began to cut the thong.

Too late.

He was moving too fast and we were too near the surrounding wall of the arena. With an effort which caused the muscles to crack in my shoulders and back, I swung him, let him go, sent him head-first to crash into the stone.

The crowd shrieked their delight as he fell, skull smashed, brains and blood showing red and grey.

As I stood looking down, the memory clicked and, suddenly, I realised what Caecina had meant when he told me to remember what I had done the last time I had fought.

With a quick movement I tore the helmet from my head, the lattice from my face. Turning to where Nero sat I raised my arm.

'Atilus!' The crowd recognised me. Their shouts were like thunder. 'Atilus! Atilus!'

I saw Nero's eyes, his sudden start. He hadn't known. He

couldn't have known. Now that he did I would surely be given my freedom.

A hope which died as I heard the warning yell from the crowd.

'Atilus! Behind you!'

A pair of Thracians were running across the sand, armed with the curved sica, carrying their small shields, intent, I realised, on my death.

Agrippinilla's work. I saw her hand rest on Nero's arm, the quick movement of her lips, her insistence as he shook his head. A warning to let me die, perhaps, her influence overcoming his reluctance.

Anger burst within me like a flame, which became a cold, relentless rage which gave me strength and added speed. If she wanted death then death she would get.

Selim was down but his net was still intact and his dagger lay close. I snatched it up, cut the thong, ran as one of the Thracians came close. I recognised him, a tiro, his companion another. Both men still had to fight in the arena, both a little unsure of themselves.

Together they edged towards me.

The trident lay where it had fallen, my sword standing in the sand close by. Weapons to hand if I could reach them, but the Thracians intended to give me no time. They edged towards me then made a sudden charge.

Agonestes had taught me how to use a net. I cast it, sent it whirling through the air towards the oncoming men. Unattached to my wrist it travelled further than they had expected. The mesh settled over a helmet, dropped over the curved sica.

As his companion paused I stooped, gathered up a handful of sand and threw it into his eyes.

Blinded he staggered back, hands lifting, afraid. Before he could recover I was on him, my left hand gripping his right wrist, trapping his sword, my right driving the dagger past his shield and into his guts.

The guts spilled out as I dragged the edge across and free.

As he fell I ran to where the trident lay in the sand.

The other man was free, scraps of net lying around him, his sica lifted, shield held out before him as he cautiously approached.

To one side lay my discarded helmet and I turned the man so that his back was towards it, thrusting with the trident at his eyes, forcing him to keep up his shield and his sword. Had he had more experience he would have blocked the tines with his sica, used his shield as a club as he moved in, but he was wary of the dagger I held in my my blood-stained hand.

'Back, you fool!' I snarled. 'Back or I'll gut you like the other.'

'Atilus, just go down. Take a fall. You won't suffer for it. They're bound to give you mercy.'

Perhaps, but he wouldn't and neither would Nero's mother.

Metal rasped as he made a sudden cut, the curved edge sliding from the tines into the wood, biting deep into the shaft of the trident. Trapped I threw it wide, advanced, the dagger lifted, thrusting.

'No!' He retreated. 'Atilus! No!'

A weakling, facing naked, blood-smeared steel, looking into my eyes and seeing death. His foot hit the helmet and he fell, helped by my shove, the sica falling from his hand.

Without hesitation I drove the trident into his eyes, the barbs grating on bone as they passed on to penetrate his brain.

Tearing it free I raised it and ran towards the podium where Nero sat.

'Your oath!' I yelled. 'Nero, your oath!'

He didn't hear me, he couldn't. From all sides came a sound unique to Rome. A screaming roar vented by hysterical women and blood-crazed men delighted at the spectacle of death and pain.

Then officials came before him and Agrippinilla, blocking my target, the flesh into which I had intended to hurl the trident.

Gallus Caecina took it from my hand. He had come running towards me and now clapped me on the shoulder, his face wreathed in smiles.

'You've done it, Atilus! You've done it!'

'What?'

'The rudis, man! You've been granted the rudis!'

Nero held it, smiling as he rose, one hand lifted for silence. His voice rose loud and clear as he made the presentation, but I didn't hear the words.

I saw nothing but the wooden sword he held, uplifted, before throwing it to me.

The rudis!

My freedom!

Around me rose the sound again, the cheers, the yells, the shouts, the cries. The noise of the people. The voice of Rome.

GLOSSARY OF TERMS

Andabatae	Men who fought blind
Bestiarii	Men who fought animals
Dimachaeri	Armed with two daggers
Eques	Fighters from horseback
Essedarii	Chariot fighters – men who fought from chariots
Gaetulians	Dart-throwers (small javelins)
Hoplomach	Greek fighters using pikes
Lanista	Promoter/Manager with own troupe of gladiators
Laquearii	Lasso-men
Ludi	Games
Lusiones	Events between *Lusorii*
Lusorii	Using wooden weapons – a preliminary to actual murderous combat
Munera	Spectacle, show
Myrmillo	Fighter based on original Samnite, i.e. sword and shield
Paegrarii	Wooden shields and long whips or any other relatively harmless weapon. Mock fights for amusement – sometimes between cripples
Postulati	Heavily armed and armoured fighters who took on all-comers
Prolusions	Fights between *Paegrarii*
Pugiles	Boxers using *caestus* – metal studded gloves
Retiarii	Net and trident fighters
Secutor	Akin to *myrmillo* usual opponent of *retiarius*
Spectati	Men who had one or more successful fights
Thracian	Small shield and curved sword fighter

Tiros (*Tyros*)	Beginners
Velite	Armed with a spear attached to wrist by thong
Veterani	Old hands

NIGEL NICOLSON

PORTRAIT OF A MARRIAGE

Portrait of a Marriage tells the story of Harold Nicolson's forty-nine-year marriage to Vita Sackville-West, a union based on mutual trust, shared interests, deepening love, total frankness and reciprocal infidelity. It is also the journal of Vita's love affair with Violet Trefusis, the crisis which nearly broke the Nicolsons' unconventional, but extraordinarily successful marriage.

'Vita's . . . journal will earn an honoured place in the records of confessional literature.'
THE TIMES

'Excels for intensity and unexpectedness anything of its kind in fiction.'
FINANCIAL TIMES

'Mr Nicolson's good faith is patent . . . the tone perfect.'
Sybille Bedford, THE LISTENER

'THE MOST CONVINCING AND ENTHRALLING OF LOVE STORIES.'
ECONOMIST

THOR HEYERDAHL

Sea Routes to Polynesia

WHO WERE THE POLYNESIANS?

When Thor Heyerdahl first suggested that the Polynesian Islands could have been colonised in prehistoric times by South American Indians who crossed the Pacific on wooden rafts, many of the experts remained sceptical. How, they asked, could the frail reed and balsa wood rafts of the South American Indians have spanned such enormous distances?

The *Kon-Tiki* expedition proved that it was possible: now, in *Sea Routes to Polynesia*, Thor Heyerdahl explores the theories behind his epic voyage, describes his subsequent discoveries and provides a fascinating insight into the islands, peoples and customs of the Pacific from the Malay peninsular to the coast of Ecuador, from the aborigines of the Galapagos to the statues of Rano-Raraku on Easter Island.

THE PALLISERS Anthony Trollope

THE PALLISERS

Set amid the swirl of London's social and political life in the 1860's, Anthony Trollope's sequence of six parliamentary novels follows the fortunes of Plantagenet Palliser, dedicated politician, heir to the greatest dukedom in Britain, and his beautiful, extrovert wife, Glencora. Interwoven with their story are those of 'Planty Pall's' colleagues and Glencora's social allies and rivals, from wily Lizzy Eustace, obsessed by her famous family diamonds, to the naif Irishman Phineas Finn and his four loves.

This saga of romance, intrigue, blackmail and even murder, originally amounted to more than a million and a half words, written for leisured Victorian readers. For modern readers Michael Hardwick has produced this single volume edition, skilfully abridged to preserve the spirit and intention of Trollope's great work.

VIZZINI

THE SECRET LIFE OF AMERICA'S NO. 1 UNDERCOVER AGENT BY SAL VIZZINI

In the course of his extraordinary career Sal Vizzini was shot three times, knifed twice, savagely beaten up and has had several contracts put out by the Mafia to kill him.

His story packs into one book enough material for a whole series of novels. As an undercover agent for the F.B.I., he was assigned to Naples where he became a 'friend' of exiled Mafia chieftain Charles 'Lucky' Luciano; to Burma, where he blew up a heroin factory; to Lebanon, where he outwitted a Communist gun-running ring; and to Atlanta, Georgia, where he posed as a con in the Federal Pen in order to find out where a million dollars in government bonds had been hidden by a prisoner.